# THE TEACHER AND THE PREACHER

## LONESTAR LOVE BOOK THREE

### VICTORIA PHELPS

Published by Blushing Books
An Imprint of
ABCD Graphics and Design, Inc.
A Virginia Corporation
977 Seminole Trail #233
Charlottesville, VA 22901

Victoria Phelps
The Teacher and the Preacher

EBook ISBN: 978-1-64563-091-3
Print ISBN: 978-1-64563-227-6
v1

# CHAPTER 1

CAROLINE

"Please, Micah, hold still," Caroline begged the baby squirming in her arms.

Micah turned his deep blue eyes to his mother's face and beamed a two-tooth grin before latching his pudgy fingers onto her collar and pulling it toward his drooling mouth. She wanted to look her best for the tea party. She was, after all, the guest of honor. At this rate, her entire bosom would be saliva soaked before she arrived.

She set the baby on his feet and took his small hands in her own. Leaning forward slightly, she let the boy toddle. Micah stepped out, leading with his chest, lifting each foot high in the air. He would walk on his own soon, and she both loved and feared the idea. At one-year, he weighed thirty-three pounds. She sighed. Would she be able to keep up with him, lift him, in another six months?

The sound of buggy wheels rolling on packed dirt pulled her attention from her son's baby steps to the street. The conveyance drew to a stop, and a tall, muscular man stepped out.

"Mrs. Connors?" he inquired.

"Yes, that's me," she answered although her stomach tightened at the lie. She was no one's missus.

The big cowboy removed his hat and held it by his side. "I'm John Wayne, Marcie's husband. I came to pick you up for the party. Marcie was busy getting ready. She sends her apologies for not coming in person."

"Thank you, Mr. Wayne." The baby squealed in displeasure at their suspended motion. He pulled on her hands and scowled.

"Call me John." He looked at the straining child. "That's a mighty fine looking boy you got there, Mrs. Connors."

His eyes strayed from Micah, to her, and back. The baby white blond, big, tall for his age. She was tiny, elfish, faery-like. Her cheek bones were high, her nose tilted and her mouth a lush pink bow. Midnight black hair was brushed away from her face revealing a widow's peak. That dramatic peak at the baby's forehead and his deep blue eyes marked him as hers. Her genetic contribution ended there.

"Micah gets his coloring and his size from his father," she answered the unspoken question. "Please, call me Caroline." She lifted the boy into her arms and moved toward the stairs.

John Wayne was by her side, cupping her elbow with his large hand, guiding her down the steps. He helped her into the buggy and waited while she arranged her skirts and set the child on her lap.

He turned the buggy and headed back up the street. "Are you getting settled?"

"Mrs. Thornton met me yesterday and took me to the rooms. There was already food in the cupboard and the bed and crib made up. It was so nice. Micah and I were both worn out from the trip." The hot, dry Texas landscape rolled by. She'd lived her whole life in Minnesota, a land of sparkling lakes and snow. Well, she'd get used to this place, and she wanted to be, needed to be, far away from anyone who might recognize her.

"Mrs. Thornton, Amanda, is my sister-in-law. She's Marcie's younger sister," John explained.

He gave the reins a shake and the horses picked up their pace. The air flowing past, hot as it was, offered some relief from the stifling heat. "Marcie lived in your rooms when she first came to San Miguel. I installed the lock on the door and the one at the bottom of the stairs. The town is not as rowdy as it once was. We have a church and our school is set to open." He tipped his head in her direction and smiled. There are more women here now, but men still outnumber them. I hope you'll keep both locks set when home." Caroline felt his sharp gaze as he awaited her answer.

"I will," she agreed. "Marcie has been wonderful. I applied to schools all over the country, but no one would hire a woman with a child. Marcie was accepting, enthusiastic, even, to have both of us. She said she would set up babysitting. I'd never encountered that word before. Micah will be staying at your home during the day and the babysitter," she rolled the word around on her tongue, "will watch both Micah and your daughter, Katie." John nodded his understanding. "Marcie wrote that there was no reason a woman with children couldn't hold a job outside the home. I can tell you, no one else shares that opinion. She said she is the midwife and sometimes doctor here. Your wife is very unusual."

John choked or laughed. She couldn't determine which. "Yes, she is certainly that."

The buggy entered a large yard in front of a white, two-story house. A porch wrapped around the building. Two women rose from a swing and met the buggy in the yard.

"Mrs. Connors, I'm Marcie Wayne and you met my sister, Amanda, yesterday." The two women beamed smiles of welcome. Caroline suppressed a laugh. They were alike as two peas in a pod with their masses of curly hair. "This must be Micah. What a handsome boy." Marcie held her hands out to the baby and, to Caroline's surprise, he launched himself into her arms.

Two children approached the little group. "These are my older children." Amanda put an arm around each child. "Tommy is twelve, and Jeanette is ten. We've engaged the services of some of the older children to watch the babies while we have our tea."

"Tommy, this is Micah. Can you take him to play with the other children?" Marcie handed the baby to the older boy. Micah grinned at her as he was borne away. Caroline gave him a little wave and sighed. He'd been so clingy on the trip, but these people had won him over at first glance. She would trust his judgment. John circled the buggy and helped her to the ground.

The frenzied barking of two dogs split the air. The dogs ran, tongues hanging, twisted in the air, and fought for the prize – a large, dirty stick. One dog was big and brown, a mutt. The other had the thick silver and gray coat of a Husky. *Poor thing,* she thought, *he must suffer in the Texas heat.* In Minnesota, a Husky was a familiar sight. They were excellent guard dogs and could pull a sled through the worst storm, but they were also loyal and loving. He was a long way from the snow, and so was she. Her stomach clenched at the memory of those cold, clear nights. The dogs pulling their sled through the falling snow while she sat wrapped in fur - warm, secure, home. Caroline blinked away a tear and straightened her shoulders.

John pointed at the brown dog. "That's Duke. He's our dog. The other one belongs to the preacher." The dogs each held one end of the stick in their mouth and were engaged in canine tug-of-war. Deep, snarling growls reverberated in the still afternoon air. "Don't worry about them. They won't really fight each other," he reassured. With a dismissive wave, John turned toward the house.

Marcie linked her arm with his. "Come in. Everyone is eager to meet you. San Miguel is a good town, and we hope you'll like it here."

The steady hum of chatter disappeared when they entered, and all heads swiveled in her direction. A lump of self-consciousness mixed with a healthy dose of fear took up uncomfortable residence in her throat. She needed this job. She needed these people to like her, but, more important, to approve of her.

Marcie led her to the front of the room. "I have the great pleasure of introducing our new teacher, Caroline Connors. As you know, the first day of school will be two weeks from today. All children between the ages of six and fifteen are welcome. Please help yourself to tea or punch and cookies."

Marcie laced her arm though Caroline's and led her to the table. She poured two cups of tea, handed one to her, and kept up a running dialogue of introductions. Caroline's hand had been squeezed until it ached, and her lips hurt from the smile frozen on her face.

A single knock on the door drew her attention. A shiver raced through her body, and she pushed it aside. She was safe. No one knew her here. Her shoulders lowered. Her fists unclenched.

"Afternoon, Preacher," John Wayne greeted the newcomer.

"Hope I'm not too late, John. I had a bit of an emergency. Granny Wilkins is poorly, I'm sorry to say." Her shoulders resumed their height. She knew that voice, but it couldn't be. Not here. Not now. Not so far from home.

"That's the preacher. Every available woman for miles around arrives at service in her best dress and stares at him like they've been forty days in the desert, and he's a glass of water." Marcie squeezed Caroline's arm. "Wait until you see him, and you'll understand."

Caroline fixed her eyes on the door. The two men entered, and blood rushed from her face to the bottom of her feet to return in scalding heat. It couldn't be, it simply could not be, but there he stood – Sven Nielson.

John motioned in her direction. "Come meet our new teacher, Sven." He stood in front of her, holding out his hand. "Mrs. Connors, this is our preacher, Sven Nielson." His giant hand engulfed her tiny one. It had always been this way. His giant to her elf, like so many of the Norwegian fairy tales they were raised on.

His hand was clammy. His eyes scorched her face. "It's a pleasure, Mrs. Connors."

"Thank you, Mr. Nielson, I..."

A disturbance at the kitchen door revealed Tommy with a sobbing Micah in his arms. "I'm sorry to interrupt the party, but Micah got mighty fussy. I tried my best, but I think he needs his ma."

Caroline pulled her hand from the preacher's grip and hurried across the room. "Thank you, Tommy. Come here, baby." She leaned down and scooped the unhappy child into her arms. Rocking back and forth, she patted his back until the sobs became sniffles. The preacher's gaze burned her back and sent her pulse racing. She lifted her eyes to his and strove for a look of defiant begging. *Don't say a word. Not a single word.*

The baby lifted his head from her shoulder and surveyed the room with those dark blue eyes before pushing his fist into his mouth.

"I'm sorry. He's teething. I've enjoyed meeting all of you, but I believe I should get Micah home." Caroline moved toward the door glancing at Sven as she went. His eyes were glued to the baby. She was out the door and moving toward town. A frenzy of conversation exploded at her back.

John hustled to catch her. "Mrs. Connors, Caroline, wait. Let me hitch the buggy."

"Don't worry. I'll enjoy the walk." Caroline called over her shoulder, but her difficulty holding the squirming child paid lie to her claim.

"I'll be happy to walk Mrs. Connors back to town." Sven's long legs ate the distance between them. He put two fingers in his mouth and a shrill whistle pierced the air. "Loki, come," he called.

The Husky stopped mid-game, spotted Sven and trotted to his master's side. "Good boy, Loki." Sven ruffled the big dog's fur.

"Loki. Oh my God. Loki," Caroline gasped. The dog studied her with his Husky eyes, blue with a ring of black, before trotting to her side and rubbing against her skirt.

"He remembers you," Sven said.

She ran her fingers through his thick fur.

"You can't carry the child all the way to town," Sven muttered. He reached for the sleeping boy. "Let me help."

He plucked Micah from her arms and laid him against his chest. He encircled the child with both arms and closed his eyes. His voice trembled. "He's mine."

"Yes, he's yours," she snapped. Anger oozed like thick mud through her words.

She stamped her foot and would have rushed ahead ignoring the blond giant except he held her son, their son, in his brawny arms.

"I don't understand. It was just the one time," he stammered.

"Yes, well, apparently once is enough." Her words, sharp as arrows, zinged through the hot, dry air.

"I'm sorry. I didn't know…" he began.

"No, you didn't know. You left. Left the next morning after we slept… no, not slept, there was no sleeping involved, after we made love by the river. At least, I thought we were making love until you disappeared. And I waited, Sven, I waited. Counting the days until I saw you again, and then counting the days until I knew I was pregnant. Pregnant and alone in a small town. The small town we grew up in. A place full of good people, but people who take rules seriously. It takes two to break one rule in particular, but only the woman gets the blame." She was walking at full speed, arms swinging.

As they neared the door to her rooms, she fumbled in her purse searching for the key.

"John said you were Mrs. Are you married?" Sven asked.

"No, in my application I said I was a widow. Marcie willing to hire a woman with a child was rare enough, but an unwed woman with a child? Even Marcie's good will can only go so far," she fumed.

"We'll get married," he declared. Sven shifted the baby to one arm and took possession of Caroline's wrist with the other.

She pulled from his grasp. "Was that a proposal, Mr. Nielson? If so, it's too little, too late." Caroline stabbed at the doorknob with her key. "Where the hell were you? Damn it, Sven, where were you?"

"Don't swear, Caroline," Sven frowned.

"Don't you tell me what to do." Caroline pushed the door open and retrieved Micah. She aimed a scorching glare up at him. "*My* baby is hungry and tired." From the wince on Sven's face he hadn't missed the emphasis on the first word of her sentence.

After delivering the parting shot, she slammed the door in his astonished face. She leaned her back against the door, tears rolling down her cheeks.

"Oh, Sven," her voice was a lonely gasp. She had cried for him, hoped he would return, prayed he would claim her and Micah. But now, when she finally had a place for herself and Micah, a place where she had a chance to live life with her chin held high, he arrived to remind her of all she had lost.

"Damn it," she repeated with more than a touch of defiant despair in her voice.

"Damn."

# CHAPTER 2

SVEN

Sven stared at the door. Loki cocked his head to the side in canine question.

"I know, Loki. That didn't go very well." He patted the dog on the head. "Come. I think we should let this rest for a bit, but," he gave Loki a firmer pat, "she was mine, before. I aim to win her back, and Micah will not grow up without his father." The declaration made, man and dog left the locked door behind them.

He walked past the small church and the smaller house he lived in and entered his workshop. He loved wood. The feel of it. The smell of it. Nothing soothed him like molding, sanding and creating with wood. He did his best thinking amidst sawdust and turpentine. Loki curled up in his usual spot by the door and watched Sven with his blue and black eyes.

He needed to finish the hope chest for a young couple soon to wed. Except for the carving, it was done. He planned on a big heart in the center of the top with the two names carved inside. Around the outside edge he would add leaves, flowers and vines. Then he'd shine the natural beauty of the wood until it was soft to the touch and a wonder to the eyes.

He picked up his small chisel and began. His mind returned again and again to Caroline. His Caroline. He had loved her all his life, and he had harmed her. He hadn't meant to, but he had caused her hurt. They planned to marry. Both families and the entire town expected it, knew it would happen, waited for the announcement. Then his brother… well, he had made his choices, too. He couldn't blame it all on his brother.

Sven had not forgotten the night by the river. He thought of it with regret, regret at all that was lost. His home, his friends, Caroline. He chipped out the beginning of a leaf.

He had gone to her house that evening as he often did. Caroline's mother said she had gone walking, so he went looking. When he reached the river, Caroline was skating, alone, in the near dark. He had stood in fear and shock as she flitted back and forth on the ice, turning circles, spinning, sprinting. She was light, and probably wouldn't crack the ice, but to go alone, at dusk, broke every rule. If she fell through, she would be gone, frozen in minutes, lost to him.

"Caroline," he had called to her. "Get off the ice. You know better than to be on the ice alone."

"I'm doing it for Micah. I miss him," she had called back. "My brother loved to skate alone."

"He died in this river – frozen to death. He was my best friend, and he was foolish. I won't let you follow him. Get off the river." Anger coursed through his veins. His jaw clenched until it ached. "I'm too heavy to come out and get you. I'd break the ice for sure." He had motioned to her, a come-here sweep with his entire arm.

When she was close to the shore, he reached out and snatched her off the frozen lake. Caroline was a feather against his brawn. He cradled her to his chest and buried his face in her black hair.

He sat on a log and stood her between his legs. "I'm going to spank you, Caroline. You knew the ice was dangerous. You knew I wouldn't want you on it."

She had squirmed in his grasp, fearing the inevitable. He had spanked her before. They were as good as betrothed, and, by tacit agreement, her father had put her discipline in his hands. Trusted him to keep her safe. It was a responsibility, an honor, he took seriously.

He had reached under her skirt, untied her bloomers, and pulled them past her knees. Caroline had struggled then.

"No, Sven, we're not married yet. It's not right," she had protested.

"We'll be married soon enough. I won't have you doing such foolish things, risking your very life. Micah wouldn't want you to follow him through the ice. He never thought anything bad could happen, but now we know it can."

With a tug on her wrist, she was over his legs. Neither her hands nor feet could touch the ground. She was that tiny. She clung to his leg so she wouldn't fall, but he had her tight against his body. He'd never let her come to harm. He lifted her skirt over her back, revealing her small, white bottom. It was shaped like a heart, and he had been struck by the beauty of it. They had spent a minute in silence while she anticipated, and he stared.

Caroline had made a little sound, a huff, a puff of air that brought him back to his task. He raised his hand and brought it down on her perfect white skin. The outline of his hand stood red against her alabaster perfection. He placed a matching print on the other side before he began to turn every bit of white skin pink, then rose, and then scarlet.

It hadn't happened before, when he had given her a smack over her dress, but he was hard and wanting her. When he was sure she would never, ever go on the ice alone, and she had promised as much over and over, he lifted her to his lap. He kissed her cheek, her neck, her shoulder. He let his hands cup her breasts and his thumbs rubbed over her nipples until they stood in stiff peaks. His hands wandered beneath her dress, stroked up and down her thighs, and found the place he'd been searching for. His finger slid into her, and she arched her back and groaned. Two fingers and she moaned and turned her face up for his kiss.

"Are you sure?" He had the smallest, most ragged control over himself still.

Caroline nodded her head, and he had lifted her to face him and lowered her onto his shaft. She made a sound of distress, and he stopped.

"Are you all right?" Through sheer force of will, he held himself still with Caroline impaled on his manhood.

"Give me a minute to get used to you. You're big all over, I guess." He had held her close and waited.

"It might be better if we lay down, but there's still snow on the ground," he had managed to explain, but her hips were moving again, and he joined the dance.

He'd walked her home. He held one hand as she tried to rub the sting from her bottom with the other.

When they reached her door, he had lifted her until they were face-to-face, and he kissed her. Kissed her with promise, hope and love.

"I'll see you soon." Those had been his last words before his brother and trouble, which were almost always one and the same, called him away.

She had been pregnant. He closed his eyes at the thought of her dismay and his betrayal. How she must have suffered. She had named the baby for her brother and his friend, Micah. It was a good name; he had been a good friend, and he was glad she chose it.

John Wayne rapped on the door to his workshop and stepped into the dusty room. His trip down memory lane faded to black.

"Hello, John. Party over?" Sven laid his chisel aside and stood up.

"It is. I wanted to check on Mrs. Connors, Caroline, to see if she needed anything," he paused. "She left so quickly, and then you ran after her like your tail was on fire. Well, it got some folks talking." John looked away and cleared his throat. "Marcie said a woman's reputation is fragile. Caroline's new to town, and, well, Marcie worries about her alone and with a baby. Caroline doesn't need the town biddies gossiping about her."

"Marcie is right on all counts." He leaned down and blew the sawdust from his carving. "Would you like some coffee? Maybe a game of chess?"

"That sounds good." The two men moved from the room. "Marcie won't mind if I'm a bit late."

"You're a lucky man, John. Marcie and three healthy children. I envy you." He slapped his friend's back in male comradery.

John laughed, "I envy me too. Those ten years I was a Ranger, I wasn't ever sure I'd see the next sunrise. Then I met Marcie. I never expected to be a family man, but I'm happy."

After he beat John twice, he moved the little table with the chess set into the corner. John stood and grabbed his hat.

"Thank you for delivering Marcie's message. I know you hate infernal interfering, as you call it." Sven held out his hand, and John clasped it.

"We'll see you Sunday." John closed the door behind him.

Sven carried the empty cups to the kitchen. He owed John a debt of gratitude. Not only for the warning tonight, but for the other times he'd acted on his behalf.

He would court Caroline. Court her proper and in a full view of the town. Much as he wanted to march up to her and insist she let him be her husband and Micah's father, it wouldn't work. She had a powerful anger built up against him, and he didn't blame her. He would have to prove himself, his devotion, his love.

If she'd let him.

# CHAPTER 3

CAROLINE

*C*aroline sat at the end of the last pew nearest to the door. Micah was with the other small children, and she wanted to be easily available if he needed her. If she were honest with herself, and she tried to be, she wanted to be as far away from Sven as possible. It was unthinkable that the new teacher would skip church, but she didn't have to be under the preacher's nose.

She suppressed a chuckle. Marcie had been right about church attendance. The front rows held well-dressed young women who dangled on Sven's every word as if their eternal souls hung in the balance. The middle rows held families and the back rows were occupied by single men and women with small children. Loki rested his head on giant paws at the back of the room. His eyes followed Sven's every move.

A handsome man in his mid-years moved to the front of the church. He wiped his hands on the sides of newly washed jeans, opened his mouth, and the most glorious music filled the church. Her heart clutched in her chest. The sound rang deep and true and vibrated from her head to her curled toes. As he finished, the congregation let out a united breath and with a collective sigh sank into their seats.

Sven rose and moved to the front of the church. He cleared his throat. "Thank you, Bill. That was mighty fine singing." He tilted his head toward the singer as he resumed his seat. "I have some announcements. Granny Wilkins is unwell. If you can find the time, she would appreciate a visitor." He leaned in conspiratorially, "We all know how she enjoys a sweet treat or two." A rumble of laughter swept the room. "The wedding of Sarah Thomas and Tad Phillips is two weeks away." He motioned at a couple holding hands near the front. "They invite you all to share the day with them. A barbeque potluck will be hosted by Sarah's pa." A middle-aged man waved his hand in the air. "Last, the harvest dance will be next Saturday." A buzz of excitement emanated from the front rows.

Caroline had heard Sven speak from the pulpit before in their hometown of Cold Spring, Minnesota. It had been understood he would replace their preacher when he retired, and she would be his wife. Well, life was a ball of yarn, and you never knew when the next tangle would stop your needles cold.

After all that had passed between them, she shouldn't love watching him, but she couldn't pull her eyes away. That powerful body, those massive hands, those light blue eyes that offered understanding, forgiveness and friendship. Sven didn't really preach. He talked in his quiet, commanding voice for ten to fifteen minutes, and when he felt finished, he bowed his head and ended the service with a simple prayer.

Sven's eyes roamed over the rows in the little church. She looked away when his gaze meandered to the back. He cleared his throat, lifted his hands, let them drop, and spoke. "Words. We use them every day, all day. To ask permission, to explain, to make ourselves understood, to connect with our neighbors and even our animals." Loki raised his head and focused his cool gaze on Sven. That dog had always been too smart by half. She stifled a laugh.

She had missed part of his sermon in her distraction. Sven continued, "Words are mighty fine, and useful, but they can be hurtful, dangerous, mean. I would ask a simple favor of you. This week I want you to think before you speak. It might become a habit." He shrugged his massive shoulders in a *why not* gesture. "This is what I ask. Before you speak, ask yourself these questions. Are your words true? Will your words injure another? Is there a good purpose to your words or are you spreading gossip?" Women squirmed and several husbands aimed heated looks at wiggling wives. "Let me just repeat that once more. Is it true? Is it hurtful? Is there honorable purpose? Is it gossip?" He bowed his head. "Let us pray. Dear Lord, Thank you for a good harvest. Thank you for health and friendship. Thank you for sending Mrs. Connors to our town and to our school. Help us be mindful of the words we speak and use them with kindness in our hearts. We ask for your guidance today and always. Amen."

Gossip. She sighed. After living in Cold Spring her entire life, after years of good behavior and good deeds, she had certainly felt its sharp edge, its cutting bite. When her stomach rounded, she had been grist for the mill. She'd always thought herself better than others, they had said. It served her right, they sneered. And, worst of all, she had driven that nice boy, Sven Nielson, from their town. She resisted a snort. You'd think she had gotten pregnant without his help—a second immaculate conception.

She returned her attention to Sven. He had closed the service, and she planned to be out the door.

That had been her intention, anyway. As she cleared the threshold, she was surrounded by parents of future students and several young men. One of whom wished to escort her across the street to the Mercantile where they gathered every week for coffee, cookies and companionship after the service.

Caroline looked into his eager face. "I'm sorry, but I have to collect my son."

"Don't worry," a woman's voice piped up, "they bring the children to the store."

"My name is Matthew," the man informed her as he held his elbow in her direction. She slipped her hand through his arm and the congregation moved to the Mercantile. Matthew had her in a chair with a cup of hot coffee and two cookies on a plate within minutes. Disgruntled looks were shared by the other single men.

The children arrived, and Micah stood next to her on his wobbly legs. When Sven entered the room, he made a straight line to her chair as if she were the North Star, and he a sailor lost at sea.

"Good day, Mrs. Connors." He held out his hand, and she had no choice but to let her small one disappear into it. Micah fell to his little bottom with a thump. His face took on the squinty look she knew so well. He was fixing to cry.

Sven reached down and scooped the child into his arms. "There, there, Micah. It's not so bad." Micah perched on Sven's arm, and the two surveyed the room, which had fallen into a hush while the congregation looked, confused and unsure, at the man and the boy. A burst of talking, pointing, staring, animated the room.

If ever a man put a stamp on a child, Sven had done this with Micah. The straight white blond hair, the high Scandinavian cheekbones, the square jaw all screamed father and son. The baby's sturdy legs, brawny arms and unusual height added to the similarities. True, the child had his mother's widow's peak and her darker blue eyes, but the resemblance to the preacher was uncanny.

In opposition to the sermon, gossip flew. Caroline recognized the hissing nastiness of it.

"But she's a widow... Marcie Wayne wouldn't hire someone she wasn't sure of, would she? It can't be."

Caroline rose from her seat and placed her cup in its saucer. She held her hands out for Micah, "I must get Micah home for his nap."

"Allow me to escort you," Sven replied. "He is far too heavy for you to carry."

She shot him a look of angry frustration, but what could she do?

17

Insult the preacher? Instead, she said, "Thank you," and walked out the mercantile door with Micah babbling nonsense to Sven and Loki following close on his master's heels.

When they reached her door, she unleashed her fury. "I don't see you for almost two years. Now you show up in the same town where I hoped to start over. You're going to ruin my life twice."

"I wouldn't have gone after Lars if I'd known you were pregnant. I thought I could catch up with him and be back in a few days, two weeks at most. Things did not go as I'd planned, and…"

"Lars, always Lars, your brother was never anything but trouble. I should have known he was at the root of this." She stamped her foot.

"Will you give me a chance to explain? Caroline, I still love you. Please, I can't let my son grow up without a father. Please." Sven's eyes pleaded his case.

"We've caused enough of a spectacle today. We can't stand out here arguing while the town watches from the door of that store." She lifted her chin in the direction of the Mercantile.

"You're right. May I take you to supper? Will you go to the dance with me?" Sven asked.

"No, to the dance. I will dance with you, but I don't want to appear as your girl." She held her arms out for the baby who eagerly fell into her embrace and laid his head on her shoulder.

"I can't commit to supper. I have plans."

"What plans?" His voice carried stern authority.

"Oh, no, you don't, Sven. You have no rights over me. We left that in Cold Spring."

Sven gave her a long look and the baby an even longer one. "Your safety and Micah's safety matter to me. I plan to court you, Caroline. I hope to regain your trust and your heart, but while I'm doing that, you have to be careful. A woman alone is easy pickings." He took a step closer. "Now, what are your plans?"

"Since you insist on pushing your nose into my business, I plan to visit the families of my students. I have been invited to several of their homes. The ones I haven't heard from, I will drop by for a short visit. It's important I have a sense of their families to be a successful teacher."

"How do you plan to get to these visits?" Sven inquired.

"The ones who extended invitations said they would call for me. For the others, I intend to rent a buggy." She tossed her head and glared.

"While I agree that knowing the families is important, homes are spread out across the range. It is not safe for you to attempt these visits on your own. Do not leave town unaccompanied. Let me know when you plan to go, and I'll take you. Caroline, listen to me on this. The west is no place for a woman to roam around unattended." He met her indignation with a scowl. "Do you understand?"

Caroline unlocked her door and pushed it open. "Micah needs his nap. Good day, Sven."

The door swung shut with a bang. As she climbed the stairs to her rooms, she heard him issuing his order still.

"Do not leave town alone, Caroline. Do not."

# CHAPTER 4

SVEN

*D*amn. The slammed door vibrated in unison with Sven's pounding heart. He would not let Caroline or Micah come to harm, and this was a solemn pledge. He hoped she took his instructions to heart, but if not, he knew what to do.

He rubbed his hands together, took a deep breath, and turned. The entire congregation stood in front of the Mercantile, mouths open, and stared.

Sven strode across the street. "Mrs. Connors is safely home," he announced. The little group turned as if from a trance, nodded, and went inside.

Sibilant sounds issued from the corners of the room, as women speculated on the scene. The sound of gossip, spitting and spiteful, was unmistakable. He sighed. His sermon hadn't even survived the walk across the street.

He finished his coffee, ate a cookie or two, and made his farewells. The single women exhaled a collective sigh and began their own journeys home. Maybe they'd have more luck catching the preacher's attention next Sunday, or, better yet, at the dance.

The following days, Sven watched for Caroline to walk by from the open door of his woodshop. He needed to talk to her – to explain. She was angry, but if she would let him explain, he thought she would understand.

When he heard the clip of a lady's boot and Caroline's voice crooning to Micah, he hurried to join her on the walkway. "Morning, Caroline," he pulled his hat from his head. "Where are you headed?"

"It's none of your business, but we plan to stop at the Mercantile. Micah is fond of the crackers they have there. I think they help with his teething. Poor little guy." She pulled a cloth from her pocket and wiped drool from the baby's chin.

Sven dropped his voice. "Caroline, I know you're angry." He held up a hand to ward off the retort he saw building behind her eyes. "And you have every right to be, but will you hear my side of the story? Please, give me a chance to explain."

"Explain." Her voice was a whip lashing the air. "Explain why you left me to the scorn of the town. Explain why you left me alone, scared and pregnant. And your poor mother, Sven, she was ill." Her chin took a jaunt forward. "How can any of this be explained?" She pursed her lips and tried to adjust Micah on her hip.

"Give me the boy." Sven held his hands out and Micah launched himself into them. "He's too big for you to manage."

"I don't have any choice, do I? I manage." Her foot stamped the ground, and she planted her fists on slim hips. If he ever tried to paint a picture entitled *Hell Hath No Fury*, this would be his model.

Micah pointed at the big Husky standing by Sven's side.

"Loki," Sven told the child. He set him next to the dog, and Micah grabbed two fists of Husky fur and held on. "Go ahead to the Mercantile. I'll watch Micah."

Hesitation and reluctance flashed across her face. "I don't know, Sven. I don't want you to get attached to him."

"Too late." He scooped the child into his arms. "Come on, Loki." He called over his shoulder, "We'll be in the workshop."

～

SVEN SPREAD a clean blanket over the dusty floor and set the baby in the middle. Loki lay down next to him and placed his big chin on Micah's leg.

"Oki," Micah patted the big dog with his open palm.

"That's right, son. Loki," Sven agreed.

Micah pulled on the dog's fur until he assumed a shaky stand. He sank to his knees and laid his body on top of the dog. His head rested on thick fur. "Oki. Oki. Oki," he chanted. Loki lay still while the baby's eyes drifted closed, jerked open, and drifted closed again.

Sven moved close and patted the child's back, "Legge seg. Legge seg." The comfort of the old language, memories of his mother's voice, soothed like warm milk and honey. "Go to sleep," he whispered, "Legge seg."

His small back rose and fell with each sleepy breath, and his chubby hands uncurled and released their grip on Loki's fur. Sven rubbed the big dog's head. He opened his black rimmed eyes, lifted his head, and let it drop back to the blanket. If the dog was content to rest with the child draped on his back, he wouldn't disturb them.

A year. He had missed a year of his son's life. Sven closed his eyes while regret swept over him with a dizzying nausea. He moved closer and laid a large hand on the child's diaper covered bottom.

Caroline's quick steps echoed on the walkway. He chuckled. She'd always been small and fast. She was a hummingbird to his lumbering bear.

He placed a finger on his lips in warning as she entered his workshop. Her face softened at the sight of the slumbering child, and the knife of regret dug deeper.

He patted the blanket beside him, and she sank to her knees. They stared in silence at the sleeping boy.

"I better take him home." She reached for the child.

"Please, Caroline. Let me explain," Sven's low voice was soaked with insistence.

"We shouldn't be here alone. People will talk. Remember, gossip?" she hissed.

"The door is open. We are visible from the walk and folks are welcome to walk in. Fifteen minutes. Please." He laid his hand on her arm.

"All right. Fifteen minutes," she conceded with a scowl.

"Thank you." He raised his eyes toward the ceiling, said a little prayer, and began, "Well, you probably remember the night I found you skating alone and pulled you from the ice."

Caroline snorted and gave a pointed stare at Micah. "Yes, I probably do." The potent mix of anger and resentment was a poisonous compound.

He flinched. "I'm sorry. I shouldn't have taken you then, or like that, but I swear it is my most treasured memory. I love you, Caroline."

She looked out the door in sullen silence.

"Well..." he continued. "When I got home that night, my mother was crying, pacing, wringing her hands. Lars was gone. Disappeared into the night with some of his no-good buddies. She'd tried to stop him, but you remember his tantrums, his anger. He grabbed some clothes, a gun, and he was gone."

"You don't even need to tell me, Sven. You were supposed to go after him, save your little brother yet again. Talk him into returning, behaving, acting like a responsible human being. Am I on the right track?"

He studied her pursed lips. Their only source of disagreement raised its ugly head. Caroline always insisted that the only person who could help Lars was Lars himself. But a lifetime of being told to watch out for his brother, to care for his brother, left a streak deep and wide. When their father passed on, he'd been twelve and Lars was seven. From that moment, he'd been the man of the family. Shoes that were always too big and rubbed his life raw.

"Well, you have the right of it, sweetheart." Her body jerked as if from a blow at his endearment. He shut his eyes into tight lines of tension. "Ma asked me to go after him and bring him home. She was ill. How could I refuse? I thought I'd catch him in a few days, a week at most, but they were traveling fast and causing trouble along the way. I've regretted that search, Caroline. If I'd known how long it would take me, the price I would pay, I would never have left Cold Spring." Sven reached out and pushed a strand of blond hair out of his son's face.

"Go on," Caroline demanded. The words were on the brisk side, but her tone had softened. He let his shoulders drop a tiny, tiny bit. Forgiveness was still a far-off thing.

"Lars and his friends committed a series of small burglaries starting just south of Cold Spring and leaving a trail heading south. More than one lawman wanted to lock the bunch of them up and throw away the key. I was always behind them, trailing by a day or two, and four months passed that way. I worried about you and about Ma, but I wanted to do as she asked. Bring my brother home." He paused and rubbed his hands on the sides of his trousers.

"I stayed in Cold Spring waiting for you, Sven. When I went to see if your mother had any news, your aunt greeted me at the door. Your mother was too ill for visitors, and she did not know where you were." A single tear trailed down her cheek. He reached over to wipe it away, but she pushed his hand from her. "I cried a million tears, Sven, and I wanted you to wipe each one away, but you were gone, and I was alone." He put his hands over his face and tried to breathe as the pain in her voice lanced him like a bayonet. "Tell me the rest," she commanded.

"I rode into Abilene. I expected the same old story, the one where I am too late to prevent Lars from causing trouble, when he and two other men burst out of the bank with guns drawn. Lars saw me and yelled for me to follow. Well, I knew whatever they'd done was bad, and I don't know what I was thinking, but I did. I followed him. They pulled up a few miles out of town. They argued. Lars wanted to split up, but he wouldn't go without his share of the money. Tempers flared. Shots were fired, and one of the other men lay bleeding in the dirt."

He squeezed his eyes shut and gathered a deep breath. "They were still arguing and waving guns, and the injured man was groaning and rolling on the ground when we were surrounded by a posse. I was arrested along with Lars and his buddies."

"Oh, Sven. How terrible." Caroline exhaled the words on a whisper.

"Yup, pretty terrible all right," Sven nodded. "Our hands were bound, and we rode back to town. They threw us into a cell. The doc came by later to tend the injured man. You know, Caroline, the truly terrible thing was Lars didn't seem to care. It didn't bother him that I was in that cell for something I had no part in. I'd tried my entire life to take care of him, and you were right all along. It never did any good." He ran a hand through his hair and down his face. "I'm mighty sorry."

"What happened then? Did you explain your innocence?" she asked.

"I tried. We were up before the judge the next afternoon. Problem was when the posse came, I was just sitting there. I wasn't trying to recapture the money or prevent them from getting away. I was sitting there hoping that somehow Lars would get clear." His laugh was a rueful cough. "I was damned lucky, though. John Wayne was in that posse and he spoke up for me. He was a Ranger for ten years, so his word carried weight. He testified that he saw me ride up after the burglary was committed. I had followed my brother out of town, but I had not helped hold up the bank."

"John and Marcie Wayne seem to help us at every turn," Caroline stated.

"They are mighty fine people," Sven agreed. "Well, the judge said

I should have been trying to get the money back, and he said that made me an accomplice. He sentenced me to six months. Lars got two years, and his buddies each got five. The two of them had been committing crimes and living on the wrong side of the law for quite a spell. Lars looked like an angel compared to those two." He looked at his hands clutched tightly together. "I was ashamed. I couldn't bear to write and tell you I was in prison, but as soon as I was released, I hurried back to Cold Spring. Ma had died without either of her sons at her side," he lamented. His voice broke, and he paused before he dared continue, "I went to your house. Your pa opened the door and took a long look at me. *"Sven," he said, "you have caused enough trouble in my house. You are not welcome here. If I see you on my property again, I will shoot you, and no one in this town will say me nay."*

"I didn't know where you were. I didn't know why your father would threaten me." His voice ripe with the pain of that long-ago rejection. Sven patted the small diapered bottom again. "Now, I do. Caroline, can you forgive me? Let me court you, so the whole town can see. Please." He laid a large, warm, hopeful hand on her arm.

"Where did you go?" Her question drew him back to the story.

"Your family took in Loki when my mother passed." He gave the big dog a pat. "It was very kind of them." His mouth rose in a rueful smile. "I collected Loki, and we left Cold Spring. I wanted to find you, but I had no idea where to look. I ran an ad in some papers around the country, but I guess you didn't see it."

"No, I never saw it." She shook her head and a lock of black hair escaped from the bun at the nape of her neck. He leaned forward and pushed the strand of soft hair behind her ear. For a moment, she laid her cheek in the hollow of his palm before lifting her dark blue eyes to his face. His heart leaped painfully in his chest. Truth to tell, another part of him was leaping and eager. He shifted in his seat.

"Where were you, sweetheart?" he asked.

"After the gossips of Cold Spring chewed me up and spit me out, I went to stay with my aunt in Winona," she began.

Sven dealt himself a blow to the temple. "Damn. Why didn't I think of that? I'd forgotten all about her." He shook his head side to side like a big dog throwing water after a swim. "Damn," he repeated.

"I'm not at all sure the preacher should swear. In fact, I remember how you dealt with bad words," she blushed.

Their eyes locked, and Sven remembered spanking her sweet bottom for her poor choice of words. From the creeping red of her face, she remembered it, too.

"I stayed with my aunt through the pregnancy. She told folks I was a widow, and that seemed to smooth the waters. After Micah was born and doing well, she suggested I get teacher training. Well, it was a good idea. I would need to support us somehow. I attended Winona National School. My aunt watched Micah. I owe her a big debt," Caroline declared and added a decisive nod of her head.

"That was smart, Caroline. I'm proud of you, and mad at me. You should never have had to worry about support. That's my job." He swallowed, hard.

"Well, you weren't there, were you?" Her words carried hurt, but she softened her voice and lowered her eyes. "Anyway, when I graduated, I applied for positions all across the country, but no one would hire a woman with a child, until Marcie Wayne. So, here I am. What brought you to San Miguel?"

"After I left Cold Spring, I wandered for a bit. Then I set my mind on thanking John Wayne for his help at the trial. John told me he couldn't stand by and let an innocent man be painted with a black brush. He was sorry the judge had sentenced me to prison at all." Sven reached for Micah who was now awake and wiggling. "He asked my plans, and I told him I had planned to be a preacher in Cold Spring, but I didn't know what to do or where to go any more. Turned out, the current preacher in San Miguel wanted to retire and move closer to his daughter. John talked to the mayor and introduced me to the preacher and the deacons. They offered me the position. It came with a little money, the little house, and this barn that I have made into my workshop. I don't believe he told them I'd been in prison, but I didn't ask." He shrugged his massive shoulders. "Thanks to John and Marcie Wayne, I've found you."

Caroline handed Micah a cracker from her bag. They watched the baby gnaw on it. Drool ran down his chin in a little river. Sven pulled a handkerchief from his pocket and wiped it clean. "There you go, little man."

Relieved of the baby's weight, Loki rose, stretched and moved to his favorite, sunny spot by the door. He dropped his big body to the ground and fixed his eyes on Sven.

"Caroline," Sven's voice a desperate growl, "forgive me."

"I'll try." She exhaled the words on a heavy sigh. "But it will take time."

Micah reached for Caroline, and Sven released the baby into his mother's arms. "All right, sweetheart. But I'll be counting the minutes until the dance Saturday. I need you in my arms." He paused. "Now, I don't mean to be pushy, but, as I mentioned before, it's not safe for a woman alone in this town, especially after dark. How are you getting to the dance?"

"Not that it's any of your business, but John and Marcie are picking me up." Her words were clipped. Her grudge was as deep and wide as the river Jordan, but a river can be crossed one way or the other – boat, barge, ferry, or a swim. Surely, he could find a way to cross to the other side of her lingering anger. He would let her fan those flames for a bit. He guessed he owed her that much, but she was wrong, dead wrong, if she figured he wouldn't be keeping an eye on them.

"It is my business. You're the woman I love, and Micah is my son. Do not be foolish, Caroline. I am here to see to your safety. Hear me?"

"For heaven's sake, I hear you." She leaned down to pick up her bag.

Micah pointed at the dog resting in the doorway. "Oki," he declared.

"Wouldn't you know it," Caroline fumed. "His first word isn't mama. It's Loki." Frustration bubbled in her eyes.

With a swirl of skirt, she marched through the door.

A small chant followed her up the street, "Oki, Oki, Oki."

Sven laughed a laugh of long held relief. He had a chance. She would be his again. He would have them both – wife and son. He would. He hoped he would.

He would pray for her forgiveness with every single breath.

# CHAPTER 5

CAROLINE

*C*aroline fastened the belt at her waist and glanced in the mirror one last time. The red ribbon she had tied in her coal black hair stood in vibrant contrast and displayed her widow's peak to full advantage. Truth be told, she was mighty proud of her hair falling long and lush down her back. Vanity was surely a sin, but a body deserved to take some pleasure in their appearance. Well, if she cared, she'd ask Sven for his opinion on vanity. She gave a little harrumph. She didn't plan to let that man get under her skin again. No, she did not.

She twisted and turned to get a look at herself in the small mirror and frowned. Maybe she should put her hair up. It might be more proper. She reached back and gathered it into a single rope before letting it fall down her back again. There wasn't enough time before the Wayne family came to fetch her for her to wrangle the thick mass into a bun.

Caroline was aware she looked young for her age, but she was the schoolmarm, after all. With her ebony hair floating behind her like a cape and her diminutive figure, she despaired at looking old enough or competent enough to control a room full of children. Well, she hoped appearances would be deceiving. Training to be a teacher had been a breeze. She hoped being one would be the same. She loved children, but some of her students would be bigger than she. She gave a most unladylike snort. It didn't take much to be bigger than Caroline Connors and that was a fact. Well, it was a worry, but she wouldn't borrow trouble until it came looking for her.

Micah sat on the floor gnawing a smooth wooden block Sven had presented to the baby as they passed his workshop the day before. The little piece was too big to swallow and sanded to exquisite smoothness. Caroline had to admit that Micah loved it, and it seemed to alleviate his teething pain.

"Ready to go?" she enquired. Micah rewarded her with a wild waving of his arms. Laughing, she plucked him from the floor and carried him down the stairs when she heard the creak of the Wayne wagon.

"Howdy, Caroline," John called. He dropped to the ground in a single smooth motion.

"Hello, Mrs. Connors," the three Wayne children chorused from the back.

"Hello, children. Hello, Marcie," Caroline answered as John helped her to sit next to his wife.

The ride to the barn dance was a short one, but John filled it with instructions for one and all.

"Ava and Adam, you are to stay in the barn at all times. If you need to relieve yourselves, find me or your Uncle Tom to take you," he began.

"Yes, Papa," they replied in unison, nudged each other and laughed.

Marcie laid a gentle hand on Caroline's arm. "The twins do that all the time. Speak at the same time; finish each other's sentences. They know if the other is ill or hurt. It's a special bond," she asserted.

John continued, "Katie and Micah will stay in the children's corner, of course. The parents take turns watching the little ones."

"Don't worry, Caroline. John and I will be there most all the time. You just enjoy the dance." Marcie gave another friendly pat.

John's sapphire eyes twinkled with merriment, but they were serious all the same. "You two," he nodded at the women perched on the bench by his side, "never leave the barn unescorted. I tend to keep Marcie by my side, but many cowboys will want to dance with you, Caroline, seeing as how single women are still in short supply. If one of them gets too friendly, you just give a wave. I have a feeling the preacher plans to keep a close eye on you," he chuckled. "But be careful, and you both look mighty pretty."

He pulled the wagon close to the entrance of the barn. The children tumbled from the back like a bundle of warm puppies.

"Ava and Adam, take Katie to the children's corner and see her settled. Mama and I will be right in," John instructed. He watched the three of them disappear through the door before lifting each woman to the ground. "I want the two of you to wait for me..." he paused as Sven joined them.

"I'll watch the women until you settle your horses," he offered.

"Thank you, Sven," John agreed. "I'll be right back."

Sven held his arms out toward Micah, and the baby leaned for him like a flower turning toward the sun. "Ladies," he inclined his head toward the door.

Caroline stopped at the entrance to the barn and stared. She hadn't been to a community dance since she left Cold Spring. Oh, how she had missed the sense of belonging. How it had crushed her spirit when the people who had been her life-time companions turned their backs on her.

She thirsted to be part of this town like a man forty days in the desert yearned for clear, cool water. Sven's eyes met her own with a twinkle of understanding.

"I want to add my cake to the other desserts," Marcie gestured toward a table laden with the best efforts of the town's women.

"We'll follow," Sven replied. "Then we'll see if Micah wants to play with the other children."

The band tuned their instruments in a cacophony of squeaking and plucking. Children ran across the floor, playing tag, laughing, sweating in their pleasure. Adults drifted in groups. Men shook hands. Women hugged and kissed cheeks. A wall of cowboys stood along the back of the barn, hands stuffed in pockets or thumbs hooked through belt loops. Legs crossed at the ankle in nonchalance, but their restless eyes belied the effect.

"Let's get a place for the first dance," John put a proprietary arm around his wife. Marcie dazzled him with a smile, and they moved onto the floor. The band started and a tall man in a brown plaid shirt moved to the front. As the music gathered speed, he called the steps to the dance and the room erupted in a swirl of swishing skirts and stomping boots.

"Those fellas against the wall are single, Caroline," Sven began. "They're mighty hungry to spend some time with a woman, and you're as tempting as sweet tea in July." Sven cleared his throat. "I'll keep my eye on you, but if one of those cowboys causes you any trouble, you holler for me."

"Honestly, Sven, it's a dance. What harm could they cause?" Caroline frowned at the big man. "Anyway, you don't have any say over me. You gave that up." When a flash of pain washed over his face, she regretted her words. She probably loved him still. She suspected she always would, but her pride rankled. He'd abandoned her. Left her pregnant in a small and unforgiving town.

"Just do as I ask. If you need me, holler," Sven repeated. The heat of his body radiated toward her like the rays of the sun, soaking through to her marrow and melting her resistance. He had Micah perched on one arm and their two faces, so much alike, studied her. Caroline would have laughed at the sight if it didn't scare her so. It seemed to her that anyone giving them even half a glance would see they were related.

"Let's get Micah to the children's corner." Caroline tried to hide her distress.

"I'll take him later, I want to hold him for a bit." Sven swooped the boy over his head in a quick dip and soar. The baby shrieked with delight. "Here comes the first cowboy," Sven growled. One of the men peeled himself away from the wall and moved toward Caroline like a panther on the hunt.

"Evening, ma'am," he drawled. "Care to dance?"

She did. She surely did care to dance. "Yes, thank you." She placed her hand in his outstretched one, and they joined a square.

Caroline hadn't had this much fun since… Well, since Sven left, and she'd learned she was pregnant. She swirled and dipped and waltzed and let life buzz through her body like she was a jar of lightning bugs. Her eyes searched for Sven whenever she had a pause before the next fella presented his hand, and every time she breathed a sigh of relief. Micah was fine. He sat perched on Sven's muscular arm laughing and running his pudgy hand over Sven's face or patting his chest to the beat of the music.

The fiddler fiddled a long, moaning note and the crowd clapped their approval. "The band needs to wet their whistles and visit that table over yonder." He pointed at the cookies, cakes, and pies. "We'll be back in, oh, twenty minutes or so." More applause let the musicians know their worth, and they smiled and gave a friendly nod as they jumped down from the little stage.

Sven had materialized by her side, and her current partner gave him a look of open hostility. His hand took possession of her upper arm and drew her away.

"I can take care of myself, Sven Nielson," Caroline fumed. She wanted to stamp her foot for good measure, but surely a schoolmarm would not do anything so childish. Her feet stayed firmly planted on the dusty floor.

Sven's voice was reasonable and calm. "Now, Caroline, I warned you. These men are hungry for a woman. Best not encourage them." His face flushed a deep red. He bent to drop a few private words into her ear. "Don't forget. I plan to win you back. You and Micah both. You belong with me."

Caroline glowered. How dare he assume such a thing. She didn't *belong* to anyone. In a huff and a swish she left the dance floor with Sven matching every stride. Dropping to a bench, she took a seat next to Marcie and held her hands out for Micah. Sven set the child on her lap, but his hands lingered on his back reluctant to let him go.

Marcie's eyes twinkled with mischief. "You're none too popular with some of the ladies," she snorted. Caroline followed her gaze to a knot of young women glaring her way. "Sven has done nothing but hold Micah and watch you. I do believe they were hoping to have a dance or two with our handsome preacher."

Sven sat next to her and held a hand palm up toward Micah who began patting the offered target. "I asked the band to start with a waltz. Will you dance with me, sweetheart?" The heat of his thigh pressing against hers sent tremors racing. Her legs quivered, her breasts felt heavy and her nipples pressed against the fabric of her dress. His ice blue eyes held her darker ones in silent acknowledgment. He knew, and she shivered in spite of the sweltering heat in the barn.

She'd always loved dancing with Sven. In spite of his size, he was smooth and elegant on the floor. When he held out his hand, she transferred the baby to Marcie's waiting arms and let his fingers fold around her own. His big hand covered the entire span of her back. The heat of his fingers soaked through her dress and her camisole to leave scalding imprints on the flesh of her back. Music filled the room, and then it was just the two of them – floating, turning, flying. If she could live inside this moment, suspended in Sven's muscular arms, she would never want another thing. He surrounded her with his strength, his smell, his masculinity, and she felt his need hot and molten. Every now and again his thigh would brush between her legs as they spun in their magic web around the floor of the barn. That moment, when his thigh opened her private space with gentle pressure, left her damp with desire. She closed her eyes and groaned.

When the music stopped, Sven pulled her close and dropped a kiss on the top of her head. "Sven, stop," she protested and gave him a little shove. "It's not proper. You're the preacher and I'm the teacher, after all."

"True enough, sweetheart, but that doesn't mean we can't be in love. I've never stopped loving you. Not for a single moment." Her hand disappeared into his big one. "The town will approve of a romance. I aim to be a gentleman, but I'd like to know my chances."

A group of cowboys entered the dance, whooping and slapping their hats on the sides of their jeans. The sheriff sauntered over and had a small word before allowing them into the barn. Men pulled their women closer and children were gathered in. These men might not be looking for trouble, but they had the makings for it.

"I believe they're a little drunk, Caroline. Stay away from them," Sven cautioned. His eyebrows formed a single line of displeasure.

Caroline nodded and followed Sven's broad back off the floor. A hand seized her wrist from behind and pulled her away.

"You're mighty young and far too pretty to be the schoolmarm," an alcohol fueled voice stated. "Now my buddies tell me you done danced with nearly every cowboy here, and I think it must be my turn." He propelled her to the far side of the dance floor.

"Let go of me." Caroline pulled on her wrist.

"Stop your squirming," he spat his answer.

Cowboys smelling of cheap whisky and cheaper cigars surrounded her. They moved in a tight knot toward a small side door. She was trapped in the center unable to see through, around, or over, but she felt the sudden coolness of fresh air and knew they had swept her outside.

She tried to scream, but her throat was tight with terror and no sound passed. Hands roamed over her, and she tried to knock them away, but there were too many, and they were too strong.

Her skirt was lifted from behind, and cool air assaulted her bottom. She grabbed at the material and heard a rip.

Tears trailed down her cheeks and soaked her bosom. No, not this. Not after all she had gone through to become respectable once again. To find a place where she could hold her head high and proud. Please, not this. There would be no recovery. She knew this beyond the proverbial shadow.

She would be blamed.

Her legs shook, her arms trembled, but she continued to push and punch at the wall of masculine muscle. Laughter and insults rained down in response. She was a fly caught in a spider web. Well and truly trapped.

A roar split the air. If she ever in her life heard a lion lift his head and bellow on a plain in deepest Africa, it could not be any louder or ruthless or welcome.

One of the cowboys was lifted by the back of his shirt and thrown against the side of the barn. He slowly slumped to sit with his legs stretched out in front of his body, loose limbed, like a puppet on a string. The second took a fierce blow to his chin that snapped his head back and sent his body soaring through empty space.

"I've got this one, Sven," a deep voice said. "I've got it, now, you can stop."

"All right, Sheriff," Sven growled.

He gathered her in his arms preventing her from sinking to the ground. "I've got you, sweetheart. I'm sorry. I should have been watching. I let you get behind me." She cried into his chest with deep, sobbing gulps. She was safe.

The one cowboy still standing tried to shake free of the sheriff's grip. "Stop that or I'll let," he dipped his head in Sven's direction, "him have a crack at you."

"We was just having a little fun. We didn't mean no harm," the prisoner began.

"Does it look like she was having fun?" Sven spat.

Caroline lifted her head from Sven's chest as the three men considered the red ribbon torn loose from her hair and hanging around her neck, the tear at the back of her dress, her red eyes and tear stained face.

"Do you boys work for a ranch around here?" the sheriff enquired.

"We're just passing through. Hoped to get a spot on a drive," the ruffian replied.

"I'll hold them in jail tonight and let them sober up. You three varmints will get out of town tomorrow and never come back." The sheriff gave the man a shake and looked at Sven. "Will that serve?"

Sven nodded before jabbing a finger at each of the three men. "If I ever see you again, you'll be sorry and that's a goddamned promise."

John Wayne stepped through the door. "Is everything all right?" he asked.

"Those three cowboys that arrived late gave Caroline a hard time. The sheriff is taking them to jail," Sven explained. Caroline still clung to him like a barnacle on the bottom of a boat.

"I'll give you a hand, Sheriff," John said. He hauled the other two to their feet. "Take Caroline home, Sven. When I'm done here, I'll gather my family, and we'll bring Micah." He paused. "Caroline, I know this was not your fault, but I think it best if the townsfolk don't see you upset and…" he motioned at her disarray. "A single woman, the schoolmarm at that, and a sharp tongue can do a lot of damage."

Caroline was lifted off the ground and cuddled against a strong chest. A sob choked her. She wasn't ruined after all. Thank God. Thank Sven.

When they reached her door, Sven lowered her gently to the ground and cradled her face in his hands.

"Please be mine. Watching you dance with those cowboys tonight liked to kill me. Their hands touching you, their voices in your ear was more than I could bear." His voice cracked.

Caroline's legs had gained a little strength, and she stepped back to look him in the eye. "I wanted to hang on to my anger. I wanted you to suffer like I did, but I guess you were in a hell of your own," she said. "Pride. When you left me, my pride took a powerful blow."

"I'm so sorry," he began.

"I know you are, Sven. I know. You've always been the only man for me. I need to stop letting foolish pride and anger keep us apart." She watched the Wayne wagon rumble down the street. "I want you, and I want Micah to have his father."

He lowered his head and claimed her mouth in a sealing, healing kiss. A heaviness settled in her abdomen, and she pressed her pelvis against the evidence of his desire.

"When? When will you marry me?" he growled.

"We'll talk. Micah is almost here."

With Sven's hands resting lightly on her shoulders, they met the wagon and took their son into their protective embrace.

"Good night, Sven," Caroline said. "I escaped one scandal tonight, and I don't want to be caught spooning with the preacher. No sense in pressing my luck."

He laughed his relief. "You're right. See you in church tomorrow?" he asked as he took her key and unlocked the door.

"Yes, see you in church." She kissed him lightly, lingering on his lips before disappearing into the building.

As she walked up the stairs holding the sleepy baby in her arms, she nuzzled his damp hair. "We're going to marry your daddy," she whispered.

Micah patted his mother's back in a show of solidarity that brought tears to her eyes.

"Oki," Micah lisped. "Oki."

"Mama?" Caroline prompted.

"Oki," he responded.

"Have it your way, little man." She laughed as she settled him in his crib. "Have it your way."

# CHAPTER 6

SVEN

*S*ven watched his son sleep. The sight stirred his heart to the point of pain. He passed an absentminded hand over that organ. A swarm of feelings—love, responsibility, devotion—swamped his body.

Micah lay on his back with one arm thrown wide and the other bent to accommodate the thumb lodged in his mouth. His head was damp with the light perspiration of deep sleep. Loki lay at the child's feet with eyes closed, but he would be alert in a moment if he sensed any danger to the little guy. Micah and Loki were thick as thieves. He chuckled remembering Caroline's chagrin at her son's first word. He agreed with her. It didn't seem quite fair.

Sven leaned back in his chair, crossed his booted feet at the ankle, and pondered tomorrow's sermon.

The Sunday after the dance, Sven had discussed the sin of pride. Sven did not write a sermon. He referenced a verse, and then simply spoke from the heart. It was immediate, intimate, and effective, he hoped. The verse that Sunday had been Proverbs, 16:18.

*"Pride goes before destruction, a haughty spirit before a fall."* From the shifting and squirming of the congregation, he guessed he wasn't the only one guilty of the charge. He knew for a fact that in the little room sat sisters who refused to acknowledge each other. Men who had been partners who turned their backs when the other entered a room. He hoped his words splintered a few hearts or prevented the hurt altogether.

Caroline admitted pride made her turn from him. She'd never stopped loving him, but his apparent desertion had injured her in that sensitive spot.

He had been guilty of that offense himself. When he was imprisoned, he should have written to Caroline and explained. She would have been angry, astonished, amazed that the law-abiding man she knew was in jail, but she would have known where he was, and how he longed for her. She would have known he would come for her as soon as he could. She would have been secure in his love. To his everlasting shame, he had abandoned her in her time of greatest need. And Lars, well, Lars was at the core of this particular rotten apple.

For years, Caroline had been upset with the merry chase his brother set for him. She warned him time and again that Lars would lead him down a primrose path to trouble, and she had been right.

It was a pattern set in boyhood. Lars would get in a mess, raise a ruckus, destroy property, and his mother would beg Sven to go to his brother's rescue. When Lars' actions landed them both in prison, he could not bring himself to tell Caroline. Nothing but pride, pure and simple.

The following Sunday, Caroline sat in the front row directly in front of the pulpit. Her appearance in the place reserved for the fiancée or spouse of the preacher raised a few eyebrows, a good share of smiles, and an audible sigh from the single women.

The following weeks he hit the first book of Corinthians mighty hard. First had been, *"Love covers a multitude of sins. (4:8)"*. He had a personal stake in that verse. His love would surround and enfold Caroline and, he hoped, bring forgiveness. It seemed there wasn't a person in the building who didn't have some such hope of their own.

Week two centered around, *"Let all you do be done with love. (16:140)"*. Then, *"Love bears all things, believes all things, hopes all things, endures all things. (13:7)"*, and last Sunday, *"Love is patient; love is kind. (13:4)"*.

As he drew his fourth sermon about love to a close, he witnessed a few chuckles barely concealed behind a hand. Several women looked at their husbands with misty eyes, and a few looked with disappointment. He'd been wearing his love on his sleeve, and the good people of the town looked on with kind and approving eyes.

He depended on the congregation's forbearance one last time when his verse echoed the theme once again. *"Faith, Hope, and Love, but the greatest of these is Love. (13:13)"*. At the end of the sermon, he announced that Caroline and he planned to marry when school let out for the Christmas holiday, and they were all invited. The warmth, the approval, the congratulations had done much to mend their hearts and set them on a road looking forward instead of back.

Two more weeks and Caroline would be his. It couldn't come soon enough for him, and that was a stone-cold fact. He needed Caroline in his life and in his bed, hungered for her every day all day. Most nights he couldn't sleep for wanting her in his arms and under his body. Most nights he lay in bed rock hard and unable to rest. He snorted. Maybe he should return to Corinthians one more time, *"Better to marry than burn. (7:9)"*.

Burn he would. They had made love once and Micah was conceived. He couldn't, wouldn't risk it. Both of them cherished the respectability, the second chance John and Marcie Wayne had provided. Two weeks... he could burn.

He leaned forward, placed both elbows on his knees and

contemplated the floor between his worn boots. Obedience would be the topic for tomorrow's sermon. But first, it would be the subject of a discussion with Caroline as soon as she returned from her forbidden errand.

Once he held her in his arms and reassured himself that she was safe and sound, he planned to take her over his knee, bare her bottom, and spank her until she glowed like a Texas sunset after a dust storm.

# CHAPTER 7

CAROLINE

Caroline tip-toed across the threshold of her fiancé's house. Partly because the baby slept, and partly because she had an inkling, a strong one, that Sven was unhappy with her.

Sven leaned back in his favorite chair, his hands splayed across his abdomen. Caroline shivered. His clenched jaw was not a good sign.

Kneeling next to Micah, she brushed the damp hair off the baby's forehead before turning her attention to the child's father.

"How long has he been sleeping?" she asked. Caroline rose to her full five feet and moved to Sven's side. She laid a hand lightly on his shoulder and a kiss on the top of his blond head.

"About an hour," Sven guessed. "I went to see you when I finished my work. When you weren't at home, I walked to Marcie's. I know how the two of you enjoy tea and talk. I was mighty surprised only the baby was there, Caroline. Micah was tired, so I brought him back to nap. Where were you?"

Caroline cleared her throat and looked about the room as if

searching for the answer Sven might find most appealing. "Now, Sven..." she began.

"Don't, now Sven, me. It's best you tell me the truth right out. I've got my suspicions, and it's best you just tell it straight." She saw steely resolve flash across his ice blue eyes.

The warmth of female fire started to burn. Lord, that man sent shivers racing up and down her body one minute and heat the next.

"Caroline?" His voice was a growl wrapped in a question.

"I went to the MacGregor ranch," she stated with an accompanying flinch.

Sven's eyebrows reached for his hairline. "After I told you not to?"

"I had to," she said planting her fists on slender hips. "Those boys should be in school. You know they should, Sven, we've talked about it. The Mason boys have been attending for three weeks, and they began late after helping their father bring in crops. Why would the MacGregor boys need all that extra time?" Caroline lifted her shoulders and dropped them with a frustrated sigh. "I couldn't let it go any longer. Those boys need an education," she huffed.

"I agree. The MacGregor boys should be in school. That's not the issue here though, is it?" He lifted just one eyebrow this time. It posed a question all by itself. "I told you never leave town alone, and I specifically told you not to go to the MacGregor place without me."

"I couldn't wait," Caroline explained.

"Yes, you could have. You should have. I told you I would take you next Saturday. One more week wasn't going to make one whit of difference in learning their letters. If," he stabbed a finger into the empty air, "you can get those two rascals to sit still long enough to do it."

"I wanted to go today," she complained.

Sven shook his head sadly. "I explained all of this to you. Mr. MacGregor is a difficult man and quick with that shotgun he keeps by the door. I've been told that since his missus passed, he's been getting ornerier by the day. He doesn't like people dropping by. I know. I've tried to invite them to church a time or two."

"But it's my job to teach the children of San Miguel. I couldn't abandon two young boys." Caroline's voice rose in her defense.

"Did I ask you to?" Sven's inquiry was soft and low.

"No, but…" Caroline began.

"I asked you to wait one week. I couldn't take you today. I promised Finn that rocking chair for his wife's birthday. Their baby is due any time. Would you have me disappoint him?"

Caroline shook her head. "No, of course not. Did you finish?"

"Yes, I delivered the chair, and they were mighty pleased, but I want to stick to our discussion." He slapped his thigh. "Did Mr. MacGregor shoot at you?"

Caroline jumped and looked to the left and to the right.

"Quit stalling." Sven's stern voice drew her eyes to his face.

"Yes, but only over my head. A warning shot, I guess you'd call it. I pulled my horse to a quick stop." Caroline bit her trembling lip. "I was a little scared."

"A little scared? Caroline, I've been scared silly waiting for you to get home. What would Micah and I do if some harm came to you? As far as that goes, what would happen to Micah? We're not married yet. I don't have any legal rights to my own son until you become my wife." He paused. "You disobeyed me. I told you not to go. I told you I would take you next week."

Micah stirred in his sleep and gave a little whimper.

"He'll be awake soon," Sven stated. "Here's what's going to happen. After Micah has gone down for the night, you are to wait for me to come and spank you. I can't let you put yourself in danger and have it go unpunished. I won't let it go unpunished."

Caroline glanced at her son before turning sad eyes to his father. "I don't want to be spanked."

"No one wants to be spanked," Sven told her. "If they did, it wouldn't be much of a punishment. I don't give many orders, sweetheart. But when I do, I expect to be obeyed. Your health and safety, Micah's health and safety, the strength and sanctity of our marriage, are the things that matter most to me in this world."

"Please, Sven, I understand," she pled.

"Do you deserve a spanking?" he asked.

Caroline hesitated. She didn't want to admit such a thing, but he was right. She deserved a spanking. Going to the MacGregor's ranch had been foolish and dangerous. "Yes, Sven. I guess I do."

"You guess?" he growled.

"I do, but I thought I could handle it." Tears surfaced and threatened to fall.

"Accept that you deserve a spanking. Accept it and learn that I will not be disobeyed," Sven stated.

"I needed to go, Sven, those boys," she wailed.

"Caroline?" His voice was low and thunderous. "Do you deserve a spanking?"

"Oh, Sven, please," Caroline cried.

Micah gave a squawk and rubbed his eyes with his chubby fists.

Loki came awake with a bark and licked Micah's face.

"Oki," the child cried. "Oki."

The big dog continued with his devotion, licking, barking, and licking again. Micah rolled to his back fat little legs kicking at the air. He turned to all fours and attempted to crawl away, but Loki held his shirt between his teeth and allowed no progress.

Sven chuckled, and Caroline joined in. Tension drained from the room at the shared amusement for the little boy and the big dog.

Caroline rose with the child in her arms. "I better take him home. He needs a bath before dinner."

"Don't forget, sweetheart. I'll be over after Micah is asleep." He reminded her.

Caroline gave a little jump to get Micah more firmly in her arms. A wave of anticipation that was part fear, part desire, swept through her body. She blushed.

"I will be the head of our home," Sven whispered into the shell of her perfect ear.

"I know," she stammered. "I want it that way."

She walked toward her rooms with the baby straddling her hip and Sven's words ringing in her ears. "I will be the head of our home."

She sighed. It might be painful at times, but Sven was a fair man. He would paddle her bottom, but he wouldn't harm her. She could relax and place herself in his care.

It wouldn't always be easy. She had a wide streak of stubborn, and they would lock horns on occasion, but Caroline yearned for his strength and his guidance like a river seeks the sea.

She would do as he asked. She would be ready for her spanking.

A tremble ran down her spine. Fear? Excitement?

She didn't know, couldn't tell, and wouldn't guess.

# CHAPTER 8

SVEN

*W*hen Sven faced difficulties, needed to think, or was troubled, he worked with his hands. Ever since he was a small boy and his father had handed him a block of wood and a piece of sandpaper it had been so. Tonight he worked on a rocking horse he planned to give Micah for Christmas, sanding, shaping, shaving away a rough spot here and there. The boy was big and strong, and he would ride the little horse with a wild vengeance. Sven chuckled at the image.

By Christmas day, both Caroline and Micah would carry his name. He closed his eyes and offered a silent prayer. Somehow, against all odds, he had been granted his most fervent desire, Caroline as wife. Micah was a bonus he hadn't expected, and he sent another prayer of thanks for the blond baby.

The boy needed his father. Of this Sven was certain. Caroline already struggled to hold him, and the child was a bottomless source of energy. Micah needed two parents to guide him, care for him, and support him. He would, of course, be in need of discipline on occasion and this was a father's duty, a husband's duty. His hand stilled, and his mind turned to Caroline.

Caroline, his almost-wife, deserved a spanking. She had placed herself in danger. He couldn't and wouldn't allow it.

Sven pictured her small white bottom draped across his muscular thighs and groaned.

The last time he had spanked her bare bottom, he'd taken her virginity. Taken her virginity on the banks of the river in the cold of the night. She deserved better. As the man, the leader of their union, he was responsible. An ache as deep as a Minnesota lake reproached him.

In two weeks, she would be his lawful wife. He would wait to take her to bed until she was legally his. He glanced at the hardness pressed against his trousers and winced. Two weeks stretched before him in an endless sea of frustration.

Sven rose, rinsed the fine dust from his hands, and turned determined feet towards Caroline's rooms. He glanced from side to side before pulling the key from his pocket and opening the door. They had conducted a careful, public courtship and given no cause for gossip, but some of the older women in town were quick to point fingers. They might think it improper for him to have a key. "Two weeks," he whispered under his breath. "Two weeks."

He climbed the stairs to the second floor of the building and entered Caroline's rooms. A fire popped friendly warmth, and her unique smell of vanilla and roses enfolded him. He sank onto the little couch and listened as Caroline soothed Micah into sleep.

"Hello, Sven." Caroline emerged from the room she shared with Micah and sat next to him. The warmth of her thigh touching his sent heat shooting to his groin. His resolve would be tested tonight. He hoped he was up to it or not up to it would be more to the point. He suppressed a groan.

She rested her head against his upper arm. Sven lifted her to his lap. Caroline snuggled into his chest and held the fabric of his shirt in her tiny hand.

"I love you, Sven," Caroline said.

"I love you, too," he replied. "I feel so lucky to have a second chance. Without you, I'm half a man, lost and alone." He rubbed his day-old beard across the top of her head.

She burrowed deeper into his chest.

"Let's go downstairs. I don't want to wake Micah when I spank you." Sven stood and carried Caroline with him.

"Sven, please," she began.

"No begging, Caroline. You know better. You already admitted punishment was called for. I expect you to behave and accept it." Sven's stern voice echoed from the walls of the stairwell.

He pushed open the door to a spare room and set Caroline on her feet. A chair with a hard seat and a straight back stood like a soldier at attention against the wall. It didn't look comfortable, but it would work. He lifted it in one hand and set it in the middle of the room.

He held out his hand. "Come here, sweetheart."

Caroline shrank away. Rubbing her hands up and down the side of her dress, she landed a plaintive look.

"Come here," he repeated, "don't make me come get you. That's not a habit I plan to start."

Her eyes wandered to the door before settling on her husband-to-be.

"Don't even try it, Caroline. If I didn't love you so, I wouldn't bother to spank you. But because you are so precious to me, I can't ignore willful, dangerous behavior." He made a come-here motion with his extended hand.

With a grimace, Caroline placed her hand into his and stood beside his legs.

Sven placed his hands on her waist and drew her close. She was so tiny. He would remember that and temper his spanks.

When his hands undid the button on her skirt, Caroline clawed at his hands. "Don't, Sven."

"Stop that this instant," he commanded.

He continued with the buttons until a gentle push dropped the skirt to the ground. "This skirt will just get in the way. It's easier for it to be off. When we're married, you'll wear your nightgown or be naked." He was working at the ribbon that held her bloomers in place. They followed the skirt to the floor. "Step out," he ordered.

A tear rolled down her perfect cheek, but she followed his instruction.

Lord have mercy, he prayed. She stood naked from the waist down. Caroline might be small, but she was all woman. Her hips flared, her legs were straight and shapely, and a nest of hair as black as night protected her female treasure. He gulped.

He lifted her and laid her over his thighs. Her buttocks formed a perfect little heart, and small dimples winked at him. With his right hand, he caressed her exposed bottom, rubbing and squeezing. He intended to spank this perfection, he surely did, but he couldn't resist the opportunity to admire and touch. In two weeks this bottom would be his, legally and forever.

Sven made another circle with his hand before delivering sharp swats to both buttocks, the top of her thighs, and the sensitive spot where her bottom curved from her slender thighs.

Caroline groaned and pressed her pelvis into his hard thigh. Sven smiled. She liked some punishment, and Sven liked to spank. When they were married, he would explore this kind of fun with her. But tonight was not about fun, and he did not want her to enjoy his attentions.

Drawing his hand back halfway, he dropped the first real spank onto her right cheek and watched the outline of his hand appear on her porcelain skin. He struck her left cheek and waited for a repeat appearance.

Caroline whimpered and struggled for freedom, but Sven pulled her close.

He laid a handprint on each thigh, on her lower bottom, and then sought for unmarked skin. But her bottom was small, and his hand was large. It wasn't long before he ran out of unmarked territory.

He began in earnest with sharp, quick spanks. Caroline wailed her displeasure and beat her tiny fist against his leg.

Sven slowed his pace allowing time for the sting to recede before applying the next spank to her glowing behind. Caroline's shoulders drooped in relief and her grip on his leg lessened.

Once more he increased the force and speed of the spanking. Caroline writhed in pain. Sven spanked until her skin was scarlet from her upper thighs to the top of her plump cheeks before he rested his hand on her flaming bottom.

He left his hand on her scarlet skin until Caroline realized the spanking had ended. Lifting her to his lap he set her with her little bottom draped between his thighs. He knew the harsh fabric of his pants would irritate her skin, and he did not want to add to her discomfort.

Caroline raised her tear-stained face, shuddered, and grabbed his shirt into tight fists. "I'm sorry, Sven," she stuttered her remorse.

"I know, sweetheart. It's over. You're forgiven." He patted her small back with his giant paw. "Just know that I will not be disobeyed. I will not order you about. I will not take offense at opinions I might not share. I want you to be your own woman, strong and confident. But if you deny me the opportunity to keep you safe and healthy, you will be punished."

He lifted her in his arms and carried her up the stairs. With his foot, he pushed the door open to the little room she shared with their son. He laid her gently on the bed, unbuttoned her blouse and pulled her arms free.

Sven gazed at her naked body. Every fiber in his being yearned for her. He wanted to taste her, touch her, and sink into her depths. He ran his hands over her breasts, and she squirmed in her delight.

He sucked in and released a deep breath. He lifted the quilt and pulled it over her body tucking it firmly under her chin.

Micah whimpered in his sleep, and Sven went to his crib and patted his diapered bottom until he settled.

Exiting Caroline's rooms, Sven locked the door and pocketed the key. He ran tomorrow's sermon through his mind as he returned to his lonely rooms.

Two weeks until his family shared his roof. Two weeks. It had become a mantra. He spent an uncomfortable night in his lonely bed remembering Caroline's porcelain skin turning shades of red beneath his hand. Two weeks would equal an eternity.

Sven walked to the little church the next morning. His breath making puffs of steam in the sharply crisp air. He started a fire in the stove as soon as he arrived. He wanted his church to be a place of comfort. Then he sat with folded hands in the first pew, gathering his thoughts, searching for calm.

At ten o'clock his little congregation drifted through the door. Not so many as on a warm spring or summer Sunday. It was difficult to make the trip in from a ranch on these chilly mornings, but Tom and Amanda Thornton were there as well as Henry and Becky Blake. Marcie and John Wayne arrived. Caroline entered, greeted friends, and took her place of pride in the front. He smiled down at these good people and offered a private prayer of thanks for the providence that brought him here, that brought Caroline here, and brought the love of community back into their lives.

He figured they expected another sermon on love. He knew he had covered the subject so many Sundays in a row it had become a bit of a joke. He being so besotted with his fiancée he could think of no other topic worthy of discussion. They would be surprised by today's sermon, but, as was his wont, he preached from the heart and about whatever occupied his mind.

"Good morning," Sven commenced. "Thank you for braving the cold to join us today. It's in fellowship we find our comfort and our strength, and I treasure these mornings spent together." A little murmur of assent rose and spread like the ripple on a pond. "I'm happy to say that Granny Wilkins is feeling much better and is up and around. She was not well enough to join us today, but she told me she wouldn't miss the wedding for all the tea in China. That wedding, Caroline and mine, is now thirteen days away." Indulgent giggles greeted his countdown. "We are looking forward to sharing that day with all of you. Arnie plans to heat the barn with a stove or two and the good ladies of the town have volunteered to host a potluck. There will be music, and I will have the privilege of dancing with my beautiful bride." Sven beamed a blinding smile at Caroline. She blushed and shifted her bottom on the bench.

He paused and cleared his throat. The congregation settled, and, as if by an invisible signal, all eyes were trained on him.

"The verse I have chosen for today is Romans 13:1. *"Let everyone be subject to the governing authorities for there is no authority except that which God has established. The authorities that exist have been established by God."* He waited while people shifted in their pews and looked right and left as if for confirmation they had heard correctly.

"I suspect it's an unusual choice this close to Christmas, but it is a subject much on my mind as I will soon become head of my household. I know most, if not all, of the families in our town place the husband, the father, at the head. In fact, any group that hopes to live, love, and work successfully together must have a leader. If not, it is chaos. Arguments rule and unhappiness follows." Sven noticed husbands taking their wives hands into their own, possessing and promising. He also noticed Caroline lift her bottom from the hard bench and attempt to sit on her right hip.

"The army, the government, your own ranches follow this principal. Someone must give the orders, guarantee safety, while others must obey. Now, here is the thorn in this particular rose. The orders must be reasonable, consistent, and fair." Sven stopped and let his eyes sweep the room.

"Let's consider the government. When the British taxed our forefathers, quartered troops in their homes, and denied them the rights due a British citizen, the result was revolution, a revolt against authority. Now I suspect the crown took a mite different view. He saw the colonists as naughty subjects, and he sent a mighty big army over to spank us." Heads nodded in agreement.

Caroline shifted to her other hip and placed a hand on the wooden seat to help hold her buttocks from touching the chair.

"Authority abused invites revolt and rightly so. My message is simple. Men, use your authority for the good. Punish with love and not anger. Women, honor your husband's desire to keep you safe and healthy. Accept the consequences of your actions and harbor no ill will but rest in the comfort of your husband's forgiveness."

Caroline wiggled and placed her hands under her bottom.

The congregation's confusion at Sven's choice of verse was replaced with knowing nods and gentle smiles. The minister had taken his intended in hand.

Sven moved to the back of the room and took his usual spot next to Loki. He liked to shake hands with the men and share a quick word with the ladies before heading over to the Mercantile for comradery and cookies.

As John Wayne filed by, he gave Sven's hand an extra shake and slapped him on the back. "Best begin as you mean to go on," he advised. His eyes twinkled as he looked down at his wife and dropped a wink.

Sven put his arm around Caroline's narrow shoulders and pulled her close. "Let's get Micah and go have a cookie."

"Only if I can stand," Caroline grumbled.

"Sitting on a spanking is usually part of the punishment but not today. I think you learned your lesson." Caroline gave her head a vigorous shake.

Sven entered the children's room and returned with Micah perched on his arm and Loki trotting close by his side.

Micah pointed at the big black and gray dog. "Oki, Oki," he shouted.

"Mama." Caroline held her hands out for the child. "Mama," she repeated.

A laugh seemed to bubble from Micah's belly. "Oki," he replied.

"Why, that little rascal," Sven said. "I think he knows what you want, and he just won't do it." He gazed into the little face so like his own. "Don't think you'll get away with disobeying your mama when you get older, little man. Just try it and see what happens. We Nielson men honor our women and try our best to be respectful." Sven tucked Caroline under his arm. "We surely do."

Micah laid his head on his mother's shoulder and snuggled before he had the last word.

"Oki," he slurred around the thumb planted in his mouth.

Loki barked at the honor of being named, and they laughed at the wonder of being a family, being together, being loved and in love.

"I thought I had lost you forever, Caroline, and life looked mighty long and sad. I am a lucky man, a very lucky man. I won't ever let you go," Sven promised.

When they entered the Mercantile, Sven selected a cookie and offered it to the baby.

"Would you like a cookie?" he asked. "Cookie?"

Micah snatched the treat with pudgy hand. "Ookie," he affirmed before pushing it into his mouth.

"Oh, for heaven's sake," Caroline fumed.

"Don't you worry, sweetheart. He knows who you are," Sven reassured. "You're the love of his life." He set a careful kiss on her furrowed forehead.

"The love of my life," he whispered. "My heart."

# CHAPTER 9

CAROLINE

*C*aroline needed help.

The wedding was in one week. One week. Seven days. She would not be ready. Caroline grabbed the pin Micah held before he could put it in his mouth and slumped to the floor beside him.

A single tear trailed down her cheek as she gathered the wiggling baby onto her lap. What did he know about the expectations she carried like a twenty-pound anchor around her neck? Nothing. He was simply busy being a baby and doing the things babies did. Grab, pull, crawl, cry, eat, poop and sleep. Oh, and refuse to say 'Mama'. Yes, there was that.

Sven told her she was asking too much of herself. He said she didn't need to sew a new dress for the wedding, but she wanted one. He said she didn't need to hold a Christmas pageant at the school on Thursday evening, but she wanted to. He said he knew a way to reduce the stress that had her snapping at him like a fishwife. It involved her bare bottom over his knee followed by a cleansing cry. He had delivered the warning, and he would follow through if she didn't get control of her temper. This she did not want.

Caroline needed help, and she knew where to get it. She folded her unfinished dress and wrapped it in a clean sheet. She changed Micah's diaper, bundled him in warm clothes, and headed for Sven's workroom. He would be sanding and thinking about tomorrow's sermon as was his ritual, but she was sure he would be willing.

"Sven," Caroline called, "please open the door. My arms are full of Micah."

She heard the laugh that never failed to bring a tingle to her spine, and his big feet crossed the room. "Caroline. Micah. To what do I owe this pleasure?" He beamed a smile at the pair and held his arms out for the child.

"Can you watch Micah for the afternoon?" she asked. "I know I've been difficult this week, but I have so much to do." She held up her hands in a sign of surrender when Sven raised a single eyebrow in disapproval. "I know, I know, I don't have to do everything. But I want to look beautiful for you on our wedding day, and I want the town to be proud of their children at the program."

"First, you could wear a flour sack and be beautiful in my eyes. I love you and not your dress. Second, the parents of the town have been very happy with your teaching. I hear a comment nearly every day about the impact you are having at the school. You don't need to be placing this burden on your shoulders. In fact, I want to carry your burdens. My shoulders are wide, and my back is strong," Sven declared. He set the baby on the quilt he kept ready for him on the floor and handed him several sanded blocks to play with.

Caroline stamped her foot. "But I want to," she whined.

"It looks like we are headed for that discussion." He lowered himself onto a straight-backed chair.

Caroline held her hands palm up as if to ward off evil. "No, please, Sven. I have a plan."

"Tell me," he ordered.

"When I fetched Micah from the Wayne's house yesterday, Marcie asked if I needed any help." She blushed. "Well, being the stubborn girl that I am, I said no. But, if you will watch Micah, I thought I'd go see if her offer still stands. Without Micah underfoot, we could finish the dress in no time. I hoped she could help me find two more shepherd costumes, too."

"Two more costumes? I thought the program was set, rehearsed, and ready to go," Sven's reply held confusion.

Caroline shrugged her shoulders. "It was, but the MacGregor boys finally came to school yesterday. The class was practicing, and I couldn't leave them out. Every child has a costume and a line or two. So, I added two shepherds. They will each say, 'Hark'. If they don't come on Thursday, we will have a few less harks, but the show will go on."

"Old MacGregor finally let them off the farm," Sven laughed. "Are they terrors?"

"No, poorly dressed and without many manners, but I think they mean to be good. They seemed eager to be in the program." Caroline raised expectant eyes to Sven's face. "Will you? Will you watch Micah?"

"Of course. I always have time for my son." His voice rang with conviction. "You go see if Marcie will help you. Be back before dark." When she nodded, he escorted her to the door.

Caroline wrapped her scarf around her neck, clutched the dress to her chest, and hurried up the main street. Tea, company, and help beckoned to her like the North Star called a traveler. She blinked away happy tears. A job, a good friend, Micah, and Sven. All of this happiness belonged to her. She gave her arm a little pinch to be sure she wasn't dreaming.

The Wayne property lay just ahead, and she quickened her steps. Marcie would help her sort this out, and she would be ready for the school program, the wedding, and the wedding night. Fevered blood rushed to her head and for a moment dizziness caused her to sway. They'd had marital relations the one time, and Micah was the result. Ma had been angry when Caroline fell pregnant and informed her there was a reason they were called marital relations. If she got pregnant after one night this time, she would have a ring on her finger and a man in her bed. She hadn't known a girl could get pregnant after one time. Her sister had been married three years before conceiving, and the whole family viewed it as some kind of Biblical miracle.

Her pregnancy had come as a shock. Not as big a shock as Sven's disappearance, but a shock, nonetheless.

A quiver ran across her abdomen and landed between her thighs. She looked forward to the wedding night – hungered for it. Caroline supposed that made her a hussy. Her mother referred to the act between husband and wife as a duty and pulled her mouth into a grim little O. Caroline thought this was one duty she'd be more than happy to perform. A laugh bubbled from the deepest pit of her stomach.

Caroline snapped back to the present. She tapped her way up the stairs of the Wayne home and lifted her hand to give a solid rap with her knuckles. Stopping the descent of her hand just before it contacted the door, she stood transfixed. She knew that sound. She understood those cries. She recognized the distress.

Marcie was being spanked. Spanked by John Wayne. Well, it must be John. Who else would have the right? But Marcie was so strong, so sure of herself, so smart. Her jaw dropped to her chest, and she stood rooted to the spot.

The spanking stopped and was replaced by low, murmuring voices. Boots struck the floor with a determined stride, and the door flew open. Caroline stood still as a marble statue with her hand raised in a knock that would never be knocked.

John's eyes opened wide, and it took a moment before he spoke. "Hello, Caroline. Is Marcie expecting you?"

"N… N… No," she stuttered. "I hoped she might help me with

my dress, but I've come at a bad time. I'll go." She turned to flee down the stairs.

"It's all right, Caroline. Come in. I'll be glad to help." Marcie appeared at the door pale of face and eyes rimmed red.

John strode down the stairs and turned toward the barn where he stabled his horses. He barked, "I'll see to the twins." The usual twinkle in his eyes had been replaced by slate gray.

Marcie ushered Caroline into the house and shut the door against the cold December day. She lifted her shoulders in a bashful shrug.

"I'm sorry. I didn't mean to intrude," Caroline blurted. "You're so smart and independent. I never imagined John spanked you."

"Well, he means to be the head of his house same as any other man," Marcie sighed. "It's been a long time, but I deserved it. When we first married, I looked at the floor more often than the sky. Once we got the hang of marriage, and I understood his expectations, the spankings almost stopped. John would never punish me without reason."

Caroline's eyes were round as robin eggs. "What did you do?" She breathed the question.

Marcie crossed the room and entered the kitchen. "Tea?" She held the pot up in question.

"Please," Caroline replied.

"Well, I guess it started a while back. John said he wanted another baby. The twins have each other and little Katie is left too much on her own. He wanted her to have a brother or sister to grow up with. He said he doesn't believe in an odd number of children." Marcie laughed.

"An odd number of children?" Caroline tested the idea.

"Right. Not one or three. But what if we have another set of twins? Do we need to have one more to even it up?" Marcie filled the kettle and placed it on the stove. "He said we'd cross that bridge when we came to it, but I'm the one who carries, delivers and nurses for a year," she sighed. "But I agree. Another baby would be a joy, and Katie would adore a sibling."

"What happened?" Caroline was riveted to the story.

"I was feeling a little low. I might be pregnant. Even though we decided to try to get in the family way, the reality of it made me a little, oh, I guess depressed is as good a word as any." She motioned to a chair, and Caroline sat.

"The twins had cabin fever, and they'd nagged me all day to take them to town. They each have a penny, and when I wouldn't take them, they asked to walk to town on their own. John and I have told them they may walk to town on their own when they are ten and not before, and the twins know that. I guess they meant to wear me down, and it worked. John had gone to deliver horses, Katie was down for a nap, and I thought what could it hurt? To be honest, I was enticed by the idea of a little time alone. I knew I shouldn't do it, but I let them go."

"Oh, no," Caroline said.

"Oh, no, is right." Marcie's laugh was rueful. "John returned early and came upon the twins walking down the road. He got the story from them right quick and turned them back towards home. When they entered the yard, I knew I was in trouble. One, I broke a rule for the twins that we had made together, and, two, he knew I meant to hide the fact. He would have learned of it eventually. The children aren't good at keeping a secret, and I wouldn't ask them to lie to their father. I was sneaky to let them go while he was away. I violated his trust." Tears coursed down her cheeks. "He spanked me, and he forgave me." She mopped her face with the corner of her apron.

"Will he spank the twins? They knew better than to ask," Caroline wondered.

Marcie removed the kettle from the stove and filled their cups with steaming tea. "No, he doesn't believe in spanking children. Only his wife." She lifted her shoulders and let them fall. "They'll be mucking out the barn for a week or two is my guess. He said there would be a few years before Adam becomes a man when he will rebel. Young men can get mighty full of themselves. He said his father kept him and his brothers so tired they didn't have the energy to cause trouble, but the woodshed was a last resort. He remembers it well. A father has to hold a son back until his mind catches up with his body." She blew on the hot liquid in her cup. "Enough about me and my poor behavior. How can I help you?"

"Well, I need help finishing my dress for the wedding, and I hoped John had two more old horse blankets we could use. I have two more shepherds to dress. The MacGregor boys came to school Friday, and I had to give them a part," Caroline explained.

"I'm sure he does. Why don't you lay the dress out on the table, and I'll go get the blankets," Marcie said.

When the door closed behind her friend, Caroline opened the sheet and withdrew the unfinished dress. It was deep rose. A color Sven loved. She threaded her needle and began attaching a row of lace around the collar with tiny, even stitches. Two more rows would stretch from shoulder to waist, and another would trim the cuffs. The hem was marked but unsewn.

Marcie returned with two blankets. "I'll sew the ties on these, and they'll be ready to go. Then I'll begin on the hem. We can get this done." Her voice was confident. Her manner sure.

"May I ask you a personal question?" Caroline enquired.

"Sure, what's on your mind?" Marcie paused in her creation of shepherd garb.

"You said you decided to have another baby. Doesn't God decide those things?"

"Well, yes and no. Many couples let God decide. But it is possible to have a say in when and how many children you have. I buy condoms from a store in Denver. They are tubes of rubber a man wears while having sex. They're not fool proof, but it helps prevent pregnancy. Talk it over with Sven. I'm sure he knows they're available."

"I will. Now I better get busy with this lace." The two women worked the afternoon away. The sun was just slipping over the horizon when the last thread was snipped.

John entered the house with two tired, dirty children. "Marcie, these young ones need bathing and dinner. They are to go directly to bed after they eat."

"All right. Come on, children." She gave Caroline a kiss on the cheek. "I'll see you in the morning when you bring Micah on your way to school." She herded the twins from the room.

"I'll walk you home." John helped her into her coat. "I'm sure Sven doesn't want you on the road alone after the sun sets."

"Thank you. I was supposed to be back before dark." Marcie wrapped her scarf around her throat and gathered her dress in her arms.

Her mind and heart were full. Her dress was finished. Her shepherds would all be clothed, and maybe she needn't get pregnant every time she and Sven made love. Now she knew it could happen that way, she wanted to have a say.

# CHAPTER 10

SVEN

S ven walked the short distance to Caroline's rooms with Loki trotting by his side. The program was tonight, and he'd promised to help ready the little school room.

Caroline had been a whirling dervish of nervous energy all week. He'd managed not to turn her bottom a bright pink, but his hand itched. He rubbed the offending palm against the side of his pants. She'd worked herself into a lather. She wasn't eating well, and he didn't believe she was getting enough sleep. After Saturday, he would monitor those behaviors for himself.

Saturday couldn't come soon enough as far as he was concerned. Caroline would calm down after they'd said their 'I dos', or he'd calm her down. One way or the other. Yes, sir, one way or the other.

He pulled the key from his pocket and unlocked the door. "Caroline," he called, "I'm here. Are you ready?"

Her flushed face appeared at the top of the stairs. "Just a minute. Would you come up and get Micah?"

"Micah? Where are you, Micah?" he sang as he climbed the stairs. It was a little game they had, the boy and he. Micah's loud screech split the air, and when Sven entered the room, the baby had thrown a blanket over his head. He wriggled on his bottom and kicked his feet in delight.

"Where's Micah?" Sven roared again.

The baby giggled and ripped the blanket from his head with a squeal.

"There he is," Sven declared. He scooped him into his arms pausing to put his lips to the baby's tummy and blow. More giggles and more wriggling were Sven's rewards.

Sven lowered the child to the ground so he could pet the dog.

"Oki," Micah gave him several thumping pats.

"Stop playing and get him ready for the cold." Caroline ordered from the door to the bedroom.

"Caroline." Sven's pale blue eyes snapped.

"I'm sorry. I'm so nervous." She wrung her hands. "I hope Margaret Foster doesn't forget to bring her baby."

"I don't believe the Fosters will forget they have a baby, but why are you worried about him?" Sven wrapped Micah in a quilt and tied the bow of his knitted cap under his chin.

"He's going to be baby Jesus. I talked to her yesterday. It will be so much more lifelike with a real baby in the manger." Caroline buttoned her coat and wrapped a scarf around her neck. She picked up a tray of cookies. "Ready," she declared and headed for the stairs.

"I thought the parents were providing the food," Sven said. "Come, Loki." He pointed at a spot next to his leg, and the dog took his position.

"They are, but I was worried there wouldn't be enough," she called over her shoulder.

The walk to the school was achieved in silence. Sven wanted the evening to go well, and a scolding on the way wouldn't help achieve that goal.

Once in the little room, Sven sat Micah on a blanket and

motioned Loki to guard him. The big dog dropped to the ground. His nose settled between his paws, and his tail thumped the ground. Micah crawled closer to get a fist full of fur. Sven grinned. A dog was a loyal friend. Sometimes better than the ones that stood on two legs, and that was a fact.

"I'll get the fire going in the stove. Until it's warm in here, you and Micah stay bundled up," Sven ordered.

Caroline, buzzing from corner to corner like a hummingbird too friendly with the corn liquor, prepared the stage, lit lanterns, and scattered boughs of greenery about the room.

Sven snatched her from her frenzied orbit and pulled her into his arms. He held her close, and felt her heart thumping against his chest. "Sweetheart, I love you; the children love you; the town loves you. Everyone is excited for the program. There aren't many social events, and it's a treat when there is one. Why, people who don't even have children in the school are planning to come." He sat on one of the chairs he'd carried over earlier in the day and pulled her onto his lap. "It's going to be wonderful." He patted her back in a soothing rhythm.

Loki growled at the sound of approaching footsteps. Caroline jumped off his lap. Sven gathered Micah into his arms. Showtime.

The town folks arrived in buggies, wagons, horses and by foot. Women and children rushed into the warmth of the room while men settled the horses. He thought a flask circulated hand to hand, but it was mighty cold. You couldn't blame a man for taking a little comfort when he had the chance.

The door flew open one last time and the MacGregor boys tumbled through.

"Jeff, Eli, I'm so happy you made it. I know your farm is a fair distance away." Caroline took each boy by the arm and led them into the whirl of students.

Jeb MacGregor appeared in the door. He held his shotgun in a loose grip by his side.

Sven approached him with a welcoming smile. "Jeb," he greeted the stony-faced man, "it's good to see you." He leaned close. "Would you mind leaving your shotgun outside? It's just a children's program. You won't need it."

The man squinted at his weapon and took a careful sweep of the room. "I guess you're right, Preacher. My boys couldn't talk of nothing else but Mrs. Connors and being in the play. Darned near talked my ear off, so I brung 'em. I'll just put this in the wagon." He returned unarmed, and Sven exhaled.

"If everyone could find a seat, we'll begin," Caroline called.

Sven took Micah into his arms and headed for an open chair.

"Say, is that your boy?" Jeb MacGregor asked. "I didn't know you had a young 'un."

"No, but he will be on Saturday when I marry his mama," Sven replied.

"Well, I'll be. He looks just like you what with that blond hair. He's big, too." Jeb's voice carried over the heads of the audience.

"Have a seat, Jeb," Sven encouraged. He suspected folks had talked about Micah's appearance before, but no one had ever voiced an opinion. Two more days and he could claim him. The baby and his mama. A smile twitched at his lower lip as Caroline helped the students into their homemade costumes. Her black hair was gathered into a bun at the nape of her neck. Two days from now he could bury his face in that forest of fine, black hair. He planned to bury himself in other parts, too, but he best keep his mind off those matters for now.

On the little stage at the front of the room, Caroline called for attention. "Thank you all for coming tonight. The children and I are very excited to have you here for our retelling of the Christmas story." She turned toward the side of the stage and motioned toward the actors. "Children, you may begin."

Ava Wayne as Mary came lumbering out with a giant pillow under her dress. Alex Blake playing Joseph held her arm and gazed at her with concern.

"Let's stop here, Mary. There must be room." He banged his fist on Caroline's desk. "Mister, we need a room. My wife's gonna have her a baby." He returned to Mary's side to a twitter of amusement.

Adam Wayne appeared. "You quit knocking on my door, stranger. Don't you know the town's full up? Everybody's come to pay their taxes, and I don't have room for the likes of you," he snarled.

"But mister, I need a room. My wife can't go no further." He motioned at the pregnant Mary who nodded and patted her pillow.

"That's right. I need to lie down," Mary added.

"I'm mighty sorry, but there is no room at the inn. If you want to sleep in the stable, you're welcome to it. I can't do better than that," Adam, the innkeeper, said.

Joseph shrugged his shoulders and looked down at Mary. "That all right with you?"

"It'll do," the pregnant Mary replied. The couple meandered off the stage and circled behind. Props were hustled onto the stage: a manger, a star hanging from a long pole, straw scattered on the floor.

Mary, minus the pillow, appeared on stage and sank to her knees next to the manger. Joseph joined her and placed a reassuring hand on her shoulder. Caroline smiled and tipped her head toward the manger, and Margaret Foster carried her three-month old baby to the stage and placed him with care in the manger. She pulled his blanket tight and patted his little belly before returning to her seat beside her husband.

Younger children entered the stage each with a mask tied over their face. A cow, two sheep and a donkey peeped through eyeholes cut into the paper. They broke into a chorus of moos, baas and hee-haws until a wave from Caroline brought the cacophony to a close.

Sven cleared his throat to keep from laughing. A few other men and several mamas hadn't been quite as circumspect.

Silence regained, shepherds filed by in a line to make a soldier proud and stood in front of the stage.

Jenny Blake draped in a white sheet with a ring of paper around the crown of her head rose behind them. "Do not be afraid," she cautioned the boys wearing capes made of horse blankets. "I have good news. Today in Bethlehem a Savior has been born. You will find him lying in a manger."

Another young girl with a paper crown rose from behind the boys, "Glory to God in the highest and peace on earth," she said before both angels sank from sight.

Eli MacGregor shouted, "Hark."

Not to be outdone, his brother raised his own voice a decibel or two over his brother's and added his own, "Hark."

Sven sent a surreptitious glance in the direction of Jeb MacGregor. Praise be, the man's face glowed like he'd swallowed a candle. He might be a bit of a curmudgeon; he might shoot at anyone who set foot on his land, but he loved those boys. He wondered about the man he might have been before his wife passed.

The remaining shepherds took control of the scene. "Let's go to Bethlehem and see what's happened," one suggested. "Yup, let's go," the other agreed and the four shepherds exited to the right.

Three children entered from the left wearing old horse blankets that had been decorated with bits of lace and buttons. These characters were clearly of a higher intelligence and rank.

One of them pointed at the star hanging from a pole, "Would you look at that," he said.

"I've never seen a star so bright. I say we follow it," the second traveler stated.

"Yup, let's go," agreed the third.

Sven wondered at the popularity of that particular line. Caroline had told him she simply explained their parts and let them find the words. Well, you couldn't argue with, "Yup, let's go." He stifled another chuckle.

The three children wandered back and forth for a few minutes before joining the others on stage. It was a bit crowded with Mary, Joseph, the Foster baby, various animals, a squadron of shepherds, two angels and three wise men.

At that moment, the Foster baby decided he'd had just about enough. His little face scrunched into a tight fist and took on a purplish hue. A cry loud enough to bring a grown man to his knees filled the room.

Margaret Foster scurried to the front of the room and retrieved the unhappy baby from the manger. She gave an apologetic smile and a shrug of her shoulders before she rescued the unhappy infant.

Now the room did rock with good natured laughter. Even Caroline wiped tears from her eyes to Sven's relief. She wanted the program to be perfect, but there was no figuring or fighting what a baby might do.

The chuckles spread across the room and just when he thought they were finished, someone burst forth another guffaw. It was cleansing, good-natured, community laughter, and Sven loved it. It was, after all, the season of joy and good-will to men.

The children waited until calm reigned and at a signal from Caroline they began to sing. "Silent night, holy, night. All is calm, all is bright." Joseph stepped to the fore and motioned for the audience to sing along, and sing they did.

It was glorious. It was Christmas spirit made real. When the room rang with "Christ the Savior is Born," Sven didn't believe there was a dry eye in the house.

Caroline appeared with the actors. "Thank you for coming. You have the most wonderful children, and they have worked hard to prepare for tonight. The good women of this town have provided refreshments. Please stay and celebrate with us."

Applause loud, long and lusty circled round and round. Caroline blushed, stepped back and swept her arm to include the children in the acclaim. At her nod, they left the stage and hurried to find their families.

Sven stayed at the back with Micah perched on his arm while Caroline was swamped with well wishes and congratulations. Her eyes sparkled and her smile spread cheek to cheek. Happiness for her success spread like heated honey and warmed his stomach. His manhood was heated by another source, and he adjusted his trousers hoping no one would notice. Two more days, and she would be his.

Two days.

# CHAPTER 11

CAROLINE

$\mathcal{C}$ aroline opened her deep blue eyes and pushed a tangle of black hair from her face. Today was her wedding day. Today she would be a bride. Today she would marry the love of her childhood and the man of her heart. Anticipation tingled. A flight of fireflies took residence in her over-excited stomach.

When she'd imagined this day as a young girl, and she and her friends had spent many a day lying in the cool grass by the river doing just that, the wedding was in Cold Spring. Her family, his mother, their school friends surrounded them with love and best wishes. They spent their wedding night in the town of their birth. Maybe Sven had rented a place in town, or maybe he had built them a cabin on his mother's land, but her dream revolved around Cold Spring, the little town named for the water that ran sparkling and frisky in summer and froze to solid ice in the winter.

She was deeply sorry her father would not walk her down the aisle. That her mother was not here to help her dress and offer advice ached like a tooth needing to be pulled. She hoped to mend the rift, but it would wait awhile. The scar of her exile still too red and raw.

John Wayne would escort her down the path to her husband before taking his place at Sven's side. Marcie would stand with her, and this new town, San Miguel, would witness and share their joy. Happiness bubbled like an underground spring. It wasn't her childhood imaginings, but it was good and honest and true to the woman she was today.

Micah stirred in his crib and his eyes popped open. He grabbed the rail of his crib and pulled himself to a steady stand. He jumped and pulled on the rail until the bed shook.

"I'm coming, Micah," she called. Lordy, he would pull that bed apart if she didn't get him out.

Caroline prepared oatmeal and guided it into her son's mouth. When he grabbed for the spoon, she let him have it. There would be oatmeal on the floor, in his hair, and some might make it into his tummy, but he needed to learn. He insisted on it. She wiped a glob from the front of her apron.

Micah twisted his face this way and that to avoid the wet cloth she held in her hand, but at last his visage shone clean. With a new diaper and fresh clothes, he was ready. John would fetch him soon, and he would spend the day at the Wayne house. They would bring him to the wedding. What had she done to deserve such friends? She closed her eyes and offered up a prayer of thanks.

A knock on the door and she scurried down the stairs.

"Morning, John. Morning, Ava," she greeted her visitors.

"Good morning, Mrs. Connors," Ava called from the wagon. "I came with Pa to hold Micah."

"Thank you, Ava." She smiled at the young girl.

Oh, how that Mrs. Connors rankled. She'd not had a choice but to assume the false title. After today, she would deserve it. Mrs. Nielson, she had always wanted to be her. She pulled Micah's blanket closer around his shoulders and handed him up to Ava.

"Marcie will be along in an hour or so," John said. "She aims to help you dress and whatever else you need to do on your wedding day." The once feared Texas Ranger blushed deep pink clear to the roots of his hair. He swung into the wagon and gave a little snap of the reins. Micah looked over Ava's shoulder and scrunched his little hand open and closed in his good-bye wave. Caroline returned it before going inside and shutting the door firmly behind her.

She reached the top of the stairs when the voice of her future husband roared, "Caroline, why is this door unlocked?"

"Don't come up here, Sven. You can't see me on our wedding day," she called.

"That's just some old wives' tale, woman. Answer my question. Why is this door unlocked?" Sven demanded.

"Marcie is coming in an hour, and, oh, I forgot. I'm sorry," she answered.

"Everybody around here knows you live alone, upstairs in those rooms. Men wanting a woman wouldn't care what day it was. Have you forgotten about those drunk cowboys at the dance? I can't let you take chances with your safety, Caroline. What if one of them was up to no good and gave your door a try?" His feet pounded up the stairs.

"Sven," Caroline pled. She knew trouble when she saw it huffing her way. "Marcie will be here…"

"In an hour," he finished her sentence. "Plenty of time for what I have in mind." He turned a chair around from the dining table and took a seat. "Come here," he demanded.

"You're going to spank me on our wedding day?" Her voice rose a decibel.

"I'm going to spank you whenever you put your health or safety in jeopardy. The west is a dangerous place for a woman, Caroline. You have to remember that and live like you understand. Until you take that reality to heart, I'll make it my job to help you remember." He released a ragged breath. "When I saw the sheriff this morning, he told me about some men in town, drinking and carrying on. I needed to see you were safe, that's all. Then your door was unlocked, and my heart fell to my boots. I just aimed to have a little kiss when you came down and tell you how much I wanted you to wife. I still plan on it, but first things first. Come here, sweetheart. You know I don't aim to chase you." He held out a big hand and waited.

"I haven't promised to obey yet," she whined.

The frown on his face spoke clear as day. "Caroline," he growled.

With a sigh, she stood next to his right leg. "I expect you to come the first time I ask." He spanked her bottom with two brisk strokes. "Over you go." He lifted her and laid her carefully over his thighs.

A cool breeze on the back of her legs signaled the rising of her skirt. His big hand stroked her buttocks, and she clenched her legs together as heat pooled between her thighs.

"That's for later," he laughed. His hand descended then, and she jerked as pain, hot and heavy, shot through her body.

"I won't do it again," she begged. "I'll lock the door."

"I just bet you will," Sven responded. His hand made swift work of turning her bottom a vivid shade of scarlet. She writhed and struggled, but Sven held her close and secure to his body. When at last he let her up, she melted into his chest and sobbed until his shirt was damp.

He rocked her while his voice soothed, calmed, and brought her peace.

"I still need that little kiss I came for," Sven declared.

She turned a tear streaked face to his and felt deep heat as his lips sealed their promise.

"I will see you at the church at two," he whispered. "When I will take you to wife."

He stood her on her feet and gave her a long, strong hug. "Two o'clock, sweetheart."

His broad back filled the door as he took his leave, but before he disappeared down the stairs he turned and considered her with warm ice blue eyes. "I love you, Caroline. I must keep you safe for Micah and me." She heard the echo of his boots on the stairs, the closing of the door, and the click as the lock slid home.

Caroline wandered to the window and watched the giant of a man who would be her groom stride down the street. In all her youthful imaginings about this day, not a single one had included a spanking. She reached back and rubbed at the sting. Her bottom hurt, but her heart sang. She deserved that spanking. Sven had cautioned her about the door before. Knowing he cared enough to see to her safety kindled a deep ache.

After washing her face in cool water, she placed the kettle on the stove. When Marcie arrived, they would have a cup of tea before transforming her into a bride. She giggled and rubbed her bottom again.

Caroline ran down the stairs at the sound of knuckles rapping on her door. She threw it wide. John and Marcie stood on the other side. John had a protective grip on her friend's upper arm. His face set in serious stone.

Marcie stood on tiptoe to kiss her husband's granite jaw. "We'll be fine now. I'll lock the door."

"See that you do," he growled. "I'll be back to walk you to church at 1:45. Do not go outside. Understand me?" He gave his wife a hearty pat on her backside.

"I do." Marcie stepped inside. "See you at 1:45, darling." She closed the door and turned the key in the lock. They stood still and listened until his boots rang hollow on the wooden walk.

"Mercy," Caroline exclaimed. "Why are the men so fierce this morning? You'd think a locked door was the most important thing on God's green earth."

"When John and Ava returned with Micah, John was mighty unhappy. The sheriff had called him over for a private talk and a warning," Marcie began.

"A warning?"

"Yes. Three men rode into town late last night and headed for the saloon. Not much of a surprise there, but they became, well, disorderly might cover it in the beginning. One of the men took a girl upstairs, and when the barkeep heard her screaming, he grabbed a gun and ran upstairs. She'd been beaten pretty badly before her rescue."

"Oh no, that's terrible." Caroline rechecked the doorknob. When she was satisfied the door was well and truly locked, she motioned toward the stairs. "I have water on to boil for tea."

The two women climbed the stairs in silence before taking seats at the small dining room table.

"Milk?" Caroline asked as she poured the tea.

"No, just a little sugar," Marcie reached for the flowered bowl and scooped some of the sweetener onto her spoon.

"What happened then? Have those men left town?" Caroline leaned forward as if willing her friend to speak.

"The bartender helped the girl into the backroom, and he told the other girls to join her and lock the door," Marcie said.

"Why didn't he go for the sheriff?" Caroline's hand flew to her chest.

"He was afraid they'd break the door down and hurt the girls. It was three men against him. He got his rifle out and laid it on the bar, but he kept on selling them whiskey." Marcie blew on her steaming liquid before taking a small sip. "They rode out early this morning, and the barkeep ran for the sheriff as soon as they were gone."

A lone tear ran down Caroline's face and landed on her bosom. When her family turned their backs on her, her aunt had taken her in. But if she hadn't, what options were available to an unmarried woman with a child? Without her aunt's helping hand, she might have ended up working on the second floor of a saloon. She shivered.

"Will the girl be all right?" Caroline enquired.

"John says so. He says the girls are used to rough treatment. Some men aren't happy until a woman cries or begs, and the working girls know better than to make a fuss at a little rough play. But he took his fists to her." She winced and shook her head. "The children are safe at the house. Don't you worry about that. John left the foreman sitting on the porch with a rifle lying over his knees until he got back."

"Well, I hope those men are gone." Caroline rose from the table. "I'll make some toast and start heating water for my bath."

When the tub was full, Caroline dropped her robe and stepped into the delicious warmth. A good soak was a luxury, and she aimed to enjoy every minute.

"Ouch," she hissed as the pink skin on her bottom met the heat of the water.

Marcie laughed, "Your bottom is pink as a prairie rose, Caroline. Did Sven spank you this morning?"

"He did. My door was unlocked. I didn't know about the trouble at the saloon, but the door should have been locked. I know better," Caroline conceded.

"John spanked me more than once over an unlocked door. I learned, though, I surely did." Marcie handed her friend a bar of soap smelling of lilacs and a wash rag. "Enjoy that tub and relax for a bit. Rest while you can. You won't get much sleep tonight."

What had her ma always told her? *There's no rest for the wicked.* Well, she didn't believe Sven had rest on his mind. The way he looked at her, mercy, it left wicked in the dust.

# CHAPTER 12

SVEN

*S*ven walked with swift purpose. He arrived at the door with the single word *Sheriff* painted on the rough wood.

"Morning, Sheriff. Any news of those three hooligans?" Sven asked.

"They drank themselves silly. Did a fair amount of damage to the saloon, broken glasses, turned over tables, money owed. Little Belinda was beat pretty badly. Doc says she'll recover." He passed a hand over weary eyes.

"They're gone?"

"Yes. They rode out about dawn. With any luck, we'll never see hide nor hair of them again." The sheriff bent to pick up several pieces of wood and placed them in the stove. "It's a cold December morning." He rubbed his hands together as if hoping for a spark.

"It is that. Well, I think I'll check on the girl. Thank you, Sheriff. I don't want any trouble on our wedding day. We've been planning this for quite some time." Sven gave an inward chuckle. An understatement if there ever was one.

"Right. I plan to be there. Well, the entire town plans to be there. We're right pleased. The preacher and the teacher," he cackled before returning to stoke his fire.

"I expect everyone is pleased to see Reverend Smythe again. It was generous of him to come out of retirement to perform the service," Sven declared.

Sven stepped through the door and took a minute to button his coat. Damn, it was cold. He'd been hot enough when he spanked Caroline's little bottom, and that was a fact. Nothing warmed a man like a white bottom draped over his lap. He groaned. He had mighty big plans for that bottom tonight. He closed his eyes. Waiting was downright painful.

Sven adjusted his pants and strode as fast as he was able to the doctor's office.

"Doc," he called.

"Hello, Preacher." A small man with gray hair and a rounded belly perched above his belt entered from behind a closed door. "I was just wrapping Belinda's ribs. She'll heal up, and the black eye will disappear. Then I reckon it's back to the saloon." The doc sank into a chair. "Doesn't have much choice, I guess. She doesn't have any family."

"Would she like a visitor?" Sven asked.

"I gave her something to help her sleep. Come back tomorrow, and she might feel more like a chat." The doc pointed at the door. "Don't you have a wedding to get ready for?"

Sven's smile was so big his face ached. "That I do. That I do."

Returning to his own house, he began heating water for a bath.

The woman who cooked and did a little cleaning for him emerged from the bedroom. "I put fresh linens on the bed," she said with a blush. "There is a pot of soup warming on the back of the stove, but I doubt you'll be hungry after the dance. Women have been cooking for days for the wedding potluck. Don't worry, it'll keep 'til tomorrow."

"Thank you, Ruth. I'll see you at the church." He waited until the door swung shut behind her before pouring the first bucket of water into the tub.

It took a good while to fill his big tub. He eyed the pool of steaming water. He did believe that if Caroline sat on his lap, they would fit in the tub together. He licked his lips. He frowned at his erect member standing proudly from his body. Tonight couldn't come soon enough to suit him.

By one o'clock he was bathed, shaved, and dressed in his best clothes. His boots were polished to a blinding shine, and his hat brushed free of dirt. He didn't plan to wear the hat in the church, but to and from. A man without his hat was a man undressed.

Sven snapped his fingers. "Come, Loki," he commanded. The big Husky trotted over, tongue hanging, and dropped to a sit by his master's boot. "Something big is happening today, and you have to be on your very best behavior." Loki's tail beat the ground. Sven went down on one knee and looked the dog in the eye. "You've been my best friend, sometimes my only friend, and it's right you should be at my side today. We're getting married. It's mighty good news for the both of us." Sven pulled a deep blue ribbon from his pocket and tied it in a big bow around his dog's furry neck. "That ribbon is the color of Caroline's eyes. Don't mess with it." He gave the dog a mighty pat and rubbed between his ears. "Good dog, Loki."

He ate a bowl of the soup simmering on his stove, and at one-thirty, he left for the church with Loki prancing at his side. His stomach roiled and the barbed wire that gripped his heart pulled snug.

A wedding ceremony was a brief one, a small blessing for the groom. She'd be his in one hour. One hour. He bowed his head and whispered a heartfelt, "Thank you, Jesus." Today he would not be the preacher. Today he was simply a groom.

John Wayne's wagon pulled up to the church. He set the brake and leapt to the ground. "Howdy, Sven. Ready to get hitched?"

"I'm nervous as a cat in a room full of rocking chairs." He pulled a handkerchief from his pocket and dragged it across his brow. "I can't wait to make her mine. The waiting is powerful hard on a man."

John gave a friendly punch to his shoulder. "It is at that, but we all lived through it." He strode to the back of the wagon and lifted his children to the ground before placing Micah in his father's care.

"Ava, Adam," the two turned identical eyes his way.

"Yes, Pa?" they asked in unison.

"Watch Katie and help with Micah. I'll be back with Mama in a few minutes," John ordered. The two men watched as each child took one of the toddler's hands. "I'll go fetch the women. Time for you to go inside and wait for your bride."

Sven pulled Micah in for a hug. "Ready, little man?"

Micah patted his father on the cheek and pointed a pudgy finger. "Oki," he said before planting his thumb in his mouth.

"Yup, Loki," he laughed. "Come," he snapped his fingers and the big dog came to his side.

His mouth dropped to his chest as he entered the church. The women of the town had decorated for a Christmas wedding. Boughs of greenery lined the aisle that his bride would walk down. A red bow adorned the side of each pew and candles formed a little circle where the wedding party would stand. He blinked back a tear and swallowed heavy emotions.

Caroline would be his wife. Today. Against all odds, he had found her and won her heart and hand. He whispered a little prayer into his son's wispy blond hair.

The church filled with friendly faces and bright smiles. A wedding was an event not to be missed, especially this one. The teacher and the preacher – he'd heard the murmurs. Two important figures who led and nurtured old and young alike. The town blessed the union, and Sven's heart gave a little leap.

As the crunch of wheels came to a halt in front of the church, Sven took his place beside Reverend Smythe. He held Micah in his arms, and Loki sat by his side straining a bit against the unfamiliar ribbon. He dropped one hand, ran his fingers through the rough fur, and Loki stilled.

The congregation stood. All eyes focused on the doorway, anxious for their first glimpse of the bride.

Marcie stepped through first. December in Texas was not a land of flowers, but she carried a small bouquet of greenery tied with white ribbon. Her curly hair framed her face like a halo, and joy in her friend's happiness shone like a lighthouse beam from her leaf green eyes.

She took her place to the minister's left.

Sven shifted Micah on his arm. The baby laid his head on his shoulder and popped his thumb into his mouth. What was taking so long? She'd changed her mind. Yes, that was it. John would appear in the door and apologize to the congregation. There would be no wedding. *"Please, Caroline, please."* The words swarmed through his mind in a circle of hellish trepidation.

Caroline appeared as if in answer to his prayer. She wore a dress of deep rose trimmed with white lace. He loved her in this color. She'd remembered. He blazed a smile down the aisle, and she reflected it back. Her black hair was brushed off her forehead and accentuated her widow's peak. The length of it swung free and fine down her back.

John Wayne held her hand on his arm and patted her fingers as they made their way past the eyes of the town. When they reached the front, John placed her hand in his before moving to his side. Sven sighed. The transfer had been made. She belonged to him-almost. He squeezed her hand, and the three of them, Sven, Caroline and Micah turned to face the minister.

"Dearly Beloved," he began. "We are gathered here in the presence of God to join Sven Nielson and Caroline Connors in holy matrimony. If there are any here who object to this union, speak now or forever hold your peace." When the moment of heavy silence passed, the minister continued. "Let us pray."

Sven faced Caroline so that Micah was nestled between them.

He circled her waist with his left arm and pulled her close. When they bowed their heads over the baby his forehead touched hers creating an arc, a rainbow, over the child. A rainbow of love, protection and trust. Under the protection of that arc, Micah could grow and explore, safe in the arms of his family. Caroline and Sven would swear to be true in a few moments, and Micah would thrive in the warmth and security of their union.

Time was ticking, and Sven realized he hadn't heard the minister's prayer so lost was he in the emotion of this moment.

"Amen," the congregation said before settling in the pews.

Marcie took Micah from his arms, and Sven grasped both of Caroline's hands in his own.

"Sven, repeat after me," the minister ordered.

Sven nodded with such force his blond hair tumbled onto his forehead. He listened with great care before embarking on his vows.

"I, Sven Nielson, take you, Caroline Connors, to be my lawfully wedded wife. I promise to love, comfort, honor and keep you for better or worse, richer or poorer, in sickness and in health, for as long as we both shall live." Sven's voice, clear and strong, rang like the peal of a bell throughout the church.

"Caroline, repeat after me." The minister provided the lines.

"I, Caroline Connors, take you, Sven Nielson, to be my lawfully wedded husband. I promise to love, honor and obey you. I take you for better or worse, richer or poorer, in sickness and in health, for as long as we both shall live." He locked his eyes with hers.

The reverend waited before breaking their spell. "Do you have a ring, Sven?" he prompted.

Sven dropped one of Caroline's hands and fumbled in the pocket of his coat. He frowned as he searched until his hand wrapped around the gold band that had belonged to his mother. He handed it to the minister.

"Lord, bless this ring, she who wears it, and he who gives it. May their lives be filled with love and faith." He settled a gentle look on the baby held in Marcie's arms. "May their children bring joy to their home." He handed the ring to Sven. "Repeat after me."

Sven lifted Caroline's left hand and followed the minister's directive. "With this ring I thee wed, and with all my worldly goods I thee endow." He slipped the simple band onto her left hand and wiped a tear from Caroline's cheek.

"You may now kiss your bride." The minister gave a command he was only too happy to follow. He pulled his wife into his arms, lifted her off her feet, and sealed his mouth around hers. Later, well, later he would take more kisses, better kisses, deeper kisses, but this was all that would be allowed for now. They were, after all, in church. He lowered her to the ground and reached for Micah.

Man, wife, and child faced the gathered witnesses. Sven's grin split ear-to-ear and Caroline blushed a pretty pink. Micah sucked his thumb while Loki rose to stand by Sven's leg. Hallelujah. She was his. Legally, physically and with God's blessing. Sven leaned down to drop another kiss on top of his bride's head when the door to the church swung open with such violence it bounced off the back wall.

A big man with white blond hair and transparent blue eyes staggered into the church. Heads swiveled from Sven to the intruder, back to Sven, a few glances were spared for the light-haired baby before returning to the glowering Vikings.

"Well, if it ain't the fallen woman of Cold Spring and my jailbird brother. Finally got hitched. I'll be damned." The invader's blood-shot eyes swept the congregation. "Bet you didn't know my golden brother was most recently a guest at the territorial prison. Well, he was. Accessory to armed robbery. That was the charge, wasn't it, Sven?"

"Lars," Sven croaked. "What are you doing here?"

"You didn't think I'd miss your wedding, did you?" He pointed a finger at Caroline. "Sven always wanted to marry her. Even when we were boys, he had his mind set. But he didn't wait to bed her, and I'm pretty damn sure that's a sin. Ain't it, Sven? Fornication, I mean. It's a sin. Makes your preacher a sinner; your teacher a trollop, and that boy," he pointed at Micah, "a bastard."

Gasps, loud and outraged, surrounded them. The hot displeasure of the town burned into his chest.

Sven tightened his grip around his wife's waist. Her trembling vibrated through his body, and he feared she would collapse. The blush drained from her face and left behind pasty white. Micah sensed the distress. His thumb came out of his mouth with a pop, and he screwed his face into a tight ball of fury. Loki surged forward with teeth bared and emitted deep, deep growls of warning. Sven grabbed the wedding ribbon tied around the dog's neck and held him tight.

John Wayne and the sheriff surged down the center aisle. They each took an arm of the intruder and hustled him toward the exit.

"I think you better come with me, young man." The sheriff's gruff voice echoed through the church before the door swung shut.

Sven stood stunned, immobilized. Marcie rushed to their side. "Come with me, Caroline. You too, Sven. We need to sit down for a few minutes." She turned toward the staring, dumbfounded crowd. "Why don't you all head on over to the reception. We'll be along." Marcie made a shooing motion as if the congregation was a flock of chickens. They began to disperse albeit with stolen glances and whispered comments.

"Let me get you some water." Marcie fetched the glass and pitcher kept under the pulpit for the minister's comfort while delivering a sermon. She filled the glass with water and handed it to Caroline.

"So, that's your brother." It was a statement. No question mark in sight. "John told me about him. How he let you take blame for something you didn't do." She gave a disgusted, "Huh."

Now that the shock had worn off, tears fell relentlessly down Caroline's face. "What can we do, Sven? He called Micah a b...b... bastard," she wailed.

"Anyone dares call my boy that." Sven waved his fist in the air in menace to this unknown insulter.

"Let's take a breath," Marcie began. "The people of this town are good hearted, and they know the both of you are fine people. We'll wait a bit and join them at the reception. If we have to, we'll explain that your brother is a mean-spirited snake."

Caroline's voice was shaky and small. "Except what he said was the truth. Ugly and unvarnished, but the truth." She sniffled. Sven reached into the pocket of his best coat and handed her a clean handkerchief. He had come prepared for tears, but he'd expected them to be ones of happiness and not shame.

"Come on, Ava and Adam. Put your coats on and help Katie. We're going to a party," Marcie declared. "Pa will be coming right along." She smiled encouragement at the newlyweds.

Sven placed a gentle kiss on his bride's temple. "Marcie's right, darling. It's our wedding day. Let's not let Lars completely ruin it." He held his hand out and was grateful when Caroline placed her tiny hand in his.

The little group marched down the street with determined stride. Sven pulled open the big door to the Livery, and they stepped inside. Stoves burned bright around the room, but the chill sent shivers racing down his back.

The food tables that had groaned with the town's best offerings were nearly empty.

Marcie's sister, Amanda, hustled over. "Those biddies," she began. "Once old Elvira Peterson picked up her dish, turned up her nose, and left, others followed. Darn them. But Jeb MacGregor and his boys are here, the Blake family, you," she pointed at Marcie, "and us. We can still celebrate." Her voice quivered, and she peeked at Caroline uncertainly.

A single man dangled a violin from his hand. The rest of the band had decamped. "Want a wedding waltz, ma'am?" he asked.

"Oh, Sven," Caroline sobbed. "Take me home." She turned her face into his chest and sobbed, shoulders shaking.

Marcie held her hands out for Micah. "This little man is going home with us as planned. You two deserve a little privacy on your wedding night."

John Wayne entered the barn and shook his head at the dispirited group. "I'll go get the wagon. You wait here."

"I'm so sorry," Amanda said. "I guess we'll all head home."

Sven put his arm around Caroline's shoulders, and they slipped into the dusk. When they reached the door to his house, he scooped her into his arms and carried her over the threshold. "My beautiful bride," he whispered.

He removed her coat, sat in the rocker he had made just for this purpose, and lifted her into his lap. This would not be the wedding night he'd imagined and reimagined. Lord knew he wanted her. He feared she probably felt his stiffness through her clothes. But Caroline was wilted, withered, lifeless. She leaned against his chest limp as a sawdust doll.

Sven rocked until his bride slept in his arms. Rising from the chair, he carried her to the bedroom and laid her on the bed. He gave a rueful glance at the plump pillows and clean sheets.

As he turned to leave, Caroline's hand shot out and took fierce hold of his sleeve. "Stay with me, Sven," she begged.

"I'll be right back. I need to talk to Lars," he said.

"It's always Lars, Lars, Lars. He's always come first with you. I hate him," she sobbed.

"Sweetheart, he's my brother," he explained the obvious. "I'll be back shortly. I have a few questions that need answering, and then I'm done dancing to his tune." Sven placed a gentle hand on her waist. Caroline turned her back and refused to speak.

"Refusing to talk to me is damaging to our marriage, sweetheart. Normally, I'd spank you for it, but you have just cause. I can't deny it. Lars has caused us plenty of heartache, but after tonight I'm done with him. You and Micah are my world." He waited. Caroline's back remained resolute.

"All right. Don't leave the house. I'll lock the door behind me."

He paused for another moment hoping she might relent and speak. When the wall of silence still hung in the air like a Minnesota snowstorm, Sven rose to his feet.

"Loki." He pointed at the floor next to the bed that held his silent wife. "Guard."

Sven buttoned his coat against the December cold and strode to the sheriff's office.

"Evening, Sheriff," Sven said as he closed the door behind him. He peered toward the single cell. His brother sat on the cot. Lars had his elbows on his knees and stared with interest at the floor between his boots. "What are the charges against my brother?"

"I had Max, the barkeep, come take a look at him. He's not the one who beat Belinda. He didn't break anything, either, but he sat and watched while his two buddies did. Max said he left money on his table before they left. So, I suppose he ain't guilty of anything except keeping bad company. Lord knows if that were a crime most of us would be in jail one time or the other," he scowled. "I'll just keep him overnight so as he can sober up. Besides, I can't put him out in the cold with nowhere to go even if he is a lowdown skunk." The sheriff gave his head a rueful shake and threw a log into the black stove. "Say, Sven, I'm mighty sorry about what happened at your wedding." The sheriff aimed the disgust-soaked words at the prisoner. "That was a damn shame."

"Thank you, Sheriff," Sven replied. "Mind if I have a few words with my brother?"

"You go right ahead." The sheriff reached for his coat and hat. "I think I'll have another look around town. Be sure those other two haven't returned."

When the door clicked shut, Sven stared at Lars through the bars. "Why aren't you still in prison?" he asked. "Your time's not up."

Lars continued to examine the floor. Well, damn, was the whole night going to be one silence after the next? The air threatened fireworks, lightning, explosions. Lars rose to his feet.

"I got out early," he snorted, "for good behavior." He approached the bars, and the two brothers hurled daggers through the bars. "Then I moseyed up to Cold Spring. I knew Mama had passed, but I was curious about the old hometown. Townsfolk told me you sold the farm." His statement held a pesky question.

"I did," Sven replied. "The money is in the bank and half of it is yours. I didn't figure you'd want to settle there, seeing as how the townsfolk were so glad to see your back. I couldn't stay either."

"Yes, well, that would bring us to the lovely Caroline Connors. Those old gossips were only too happy to tell me she left town in the family way. Only as good as she should be. Pride goeth before a fall, all that malarkey." Lars shifted his weight and brought his hands to his hips. "It didn't take a genius to figure who the father would be, but I got a good look at the kid yesterday. He's yours all right. Can't figure how the good people of this town didn't know. It's plain as the nose on your face." His mouth turned down in an ugly sneer. "Not so high and mighty now, big brother?"

"How did you find me?" he queried.

"Well, seeing as how you'd sold the farm, I had time to wander around. Remembered the name John Wayne, and how he stuck up for you at the trial," he said.

The memory sent hot waves of anger pulsing in a wave of fury. John Wayne, a stranger, had taken his side when his own brother hadn't. Lars would have let the court believe Sven equally responsible for the robbery. Hell, he'd only arrived in time to get swept up in the mess. He'd not been any part of it. The memory scalded like boiling water on bare skin.

"I made a few enquiries. John Wayne is a famous fella – ex-Ranger and now breeding the best horses around." Lars paused and took a step closer to the bars. "Followed a hunch, and there you were. Respectable and about to get hitched. Landing on your feet like a cat with nine lives."

The two men strained toward one another, muscles flexed, and hands curled into fists.

"Why?" Sven's voice was deadly, dangerous.

"Why what?" Lars shrugged a shoulder in a pretense of disinterest.

"Why did you ruin our wedding? What possible excuse could there be for such meanness?" Sven asked. "My whole life I've tried to take care of you. Keep you out of trouble."

"Well, that's just it, ain't it?" Lars snarled. "Sven the golden boy, the favorite, always having to rescue bad boy Lars. Don't you ever get tired of being so goddamned holy?"

Sven stuttered, "You're jealous? Of all the stupid..." Disbelief writ large on his astonished face.

"Not jealous. Just tired to my very bones of playing second fiddle to the wonderful Sven Nielson. I could never live up to you. Why, sainthood is damn near impossible. Saint Sven," Lars snorted. "Anyway, you ain't no saint. Got that little virgin in the family way and skedaddled."

"I didn't skedaddle. I followed you. Mama asked me to find you. Keep you out of trouble, but I arrived a mite too late," Sven said. "After I got out of jail, I went looking for Caroline. It was pure luck that I found her and Micah here in San Miguel. First I knew I had a son." He cleared his throat. "We both worked hard for a second chance. Thought we could live a good life in this town, but you did your best to destroy it. Pretty sure that second chance is gone. Caroline always said you were plain mean. She tried to get me to stop chasing after you, fixing your problems, pulling you out of one scrape after the next. Damn if she didn't have the right of it." Sven heaved a sigh that held years of regret.

Lars glared through the bars. "Welcome to the world of losers, Brother."

Putting his hand into the pocket of his jacket, he retrieved a key. "This is the key to rooms above Doc's old office. Caroline lived there until today. You can stay there until you move on."

"Still taking care of me, Sven?" Lars laugh held a canyon of scorn.

"I won't have you freeze to death on the range," Sven replied.

"Thank you, Sven. You should have been a St. Bernard with a keg of rum around your neck. You say hello to that pretty bride of yours and your bastard boy."

"Micah is not a b…" Sven stopped. He would not rise to the bait. "Goodbye, Lars. I'm done chasing after you."

"We'll see about that, big brother. I don't think you can help yourself. Saving me is bred in your bones," Lars yelled at his departing back.

Laughter, scornful, derisive, mocking, assaulted the air.

He returned to his bride. Caroline lay still as a corpse except for an occasional hiccup and the shaking of her shoulders. She wept still. His heart contracted into a painful fist.

"Caroline?" Her name a question with no answer.

"I'm done with him, sweetheart. Should have been finished years ago. I'm sorry. Please talk to me," Sven pleaded.

If silence had a voice, it was screaming, screeching, wailing.

Sven hung his head. He deserved it. He truly did. But she was his wife, and they would need to figure a way forward.

He had lost a brother on this day.

He would not lose a wife.

He lay down next to his bride. "I'm back, sweetheart. Are you all right?" He ran his hand up and down her spine. "Caroline, please talk to me."

She turned her back to him. Her breathing was so shallow her chest barely moved. Sven turned on his side and cupped her bottom with his legs. "All right, sweetheart. Sleep. Things will look better in the morning."

But they didn't.

Sven woke and visited the outhouse. He washed, dressed, and prepared a plate of scrambled eggs and toast. "Come have breakfast, sweetheart." He entered the bedroom and peered over her shoulder. He didn't believe she'd moved all night long. She lay on her side, eyes closed, barely breathing. "Come on. We need to eat and fetch Micah. He'll be looking for us." Sven placed his hand on her shoulder and gave a little pull. Caroline fell onto her back. She opened her deep blue eyes and considered his face before throwing her arm over her eyes to block out the morning light.

"Don't touch me." Her voice was a razor.

"What?" he demanded.

"I believe you heard me the first time," she rasped.

Sven sat down at the table he had made with his own hands and stared at the two plates of food. Caroline was always a lively little thing, flitting here and there like a hummingbird seeking nectar. She was sunny and bright. That snarling woman lying in his bed was not Caroline – not his Caroline, anyway. He heard shuffling steps and hoped she planned to join him.

He ate his breakfast. Each bite sticking in his throat like sawdust. He left her plate on the table and returned to their bedroom. Caroline lay on the bed. Her deep rose wedding dress was twisted and wrinkled. If they were on friendly terms, he might have teased her - looks like you slept in your clothes, he'd say. One quick look at the back she'd turned to him, and he knew teasing was a bad idea. A very bad idea.

A chamber pot sat half-full beside the bed. Well, that accounted for the moving around. "I'll empty this for you, sweetheart." He carried the little bowl to the outhouse, rinsed it at the pump, and replaced it under the bed.

Sven sat alone in his two-person rocker. His hands lay loose on his thighs. He needed help. He closed his eyes, cleared his mind, and waited. He repeated his questions. What should he do about his hurt and angry wife? How could he repair the damage done? How could he help her heal?

A proverb floated into his mind. An answer, he was sure, to his prayer. *All good things come to those who wait.* Patience. He would surround her with love and patience, and she would return to him. "Thank you," he said.

Standing in the bedroom door, he watched her silence. She

probably wanted to scream at him or maybe even chuck a few dishes his way. He understood. She was mad he went to see Lars last night, but mostly she was angry at the loss of the respectability they had earned in San Miguel, their precious second chance. Truth be told, he didn't know how the town would take the revelations so brutally hurled at their wedding. Maybe there would be forgiveness. Only time would tell. More patience. He grimaced.

"I'm going for Micah," he announced. He pulled on his coat and wrapped a scarf around his neck although he didn't have much doubt that the heat of his frustrated body would keep him warm.

Loki trotted to the door, tongue hanging out and tail wagging. "Sorry, Loki." He stroked down his back before pointing at the floor. "Guard." The dog gave a whine in protest but lay down on the floor. "Thank you, friend." Sven ruffled the fur between his ears.

The door to the Wayne home swung open at his knock. "Morning, Marcie," he greeted.

"Come in out of the cold," Marcie replied. "Micah and Katie are playing in the front room."

Micah sat on his bottom while Katie explained the use of her various toys. When he saw Sven, he twisted until he was on all fours and scurried across the floor. He grabbed Sven's pant leg and pulled to a stand.

"That boy will be walking soon," Marcie chortled.

Sven scooped the child into his arms. "We'd best be heading home."

"Is everything all right?" Marcie asked. "I don't mean to pry, but…"

"Caroline is tired and still a mite upset about Lars and yesterday, but I guess we'll manage," he said. He kept his voice calm and reassuring. No point in upsetting the little man.

"Tell Caroline I'd love for her to come for tea and talk, as John calls it." Marcie handed Sven Micah's jacket.

"I'll do that," Sven agreed. "Thank you for watching Micah."

"Any time. We adore the boy, and I mean that," Marcie replied.

When he returned to his house, he stood on the doorstep. Maybe he should throw his hat in first. He laughed and Micah chuckled along. He was a good-natured boy, and Sven was grateful. He entered his home and glanced about. Caroline had eaten her breakfast and tidied the kitchen. He sighed. Maybe the tempest had passed. She emerged from the bedroom in a dark gray, wool skirt and light blue blouse.

"You look mighty pretty." He leaned down to plant a kiss on her cheek, but she dodged his approaching lips. Caroline held her hands toward Micah who fell into her arms and nuzzled into her neck. Sven felt a little surge of jealousy. He'd like his mouth on her neck, on her breasts, on her... well, on her. He would be patient, but it wasn't going to be easy. He wanted her.

His manhood rebelled at the delay.

"I'll be in my workshop if you need me," Sven said. "Would you like me to take Micah with me?"

Her small back was ramrod straight. She gave no answer but walked away with their child in her arms.

When hunger drove him back to the house for dinner, he found a sandwich ready on the table. Voices came from the baby's room, but he ate alone, sad and sick at heart.

Supper was a silent, surly affair. The only happy sounds came from Micah, cooing and patting the table with an impatient hand when he wanted more food. That night Caroline took up her position, back firmly turned. He sensed a quiet dare – touch me at your own peril. He didn't take the dare.

Three days – three long days of Caroline's silent wall. The future stretched before him in an endless stream of defiant quiet. This was not the marriage either of them wanted, and yet he felt the vise of habit falling like a guillotine blade. This would not be their marriage.

Sven prepared Micah for the outside. "I'm taking Micah to the Waynes' for a bit." He watched as Caroline struggled to keep her tongue still. "When I get back, we'll talk." He gave the usual command to an unhappy Loki before striding out the door with the baby perched on his arm.

Sven slowed his pace on the return trip. Taking several deep breaths, he opened his mind and asked the nagging question – what should he do? He needed to be calm and reassuring. Caroline had suffered a blow. A blow to her pride, her stability, her future. It was up to him as head of his household to restore hope and establish his role as a reliable, consistent leader. This was early days for them, and he must not fail. He closed his eyes and opened his heart for an answer. Relief, cool and peaceful, flooded his body like a fresh summer breeze. "Thank you," he whispered.

Caroline stood in front of the sink scrubbing at a pot. From the vigor of her attack he didn't figure that pan stood a chance. Walking up behind her, he wrapped her in his arms and stilled her frantic hands. He lifted her in his bear hug and began walking. She stiffened in his arms. "Sh," he crooned in her ear, "relax. We're going to work this out."

Sven took his place in the big rocker and set his wife on his knee. When she tried to bolt from the spot, he put both hands on her tiny waist and held firm. "No, no more ignoring me, Caroline. I won't have it."

Caroline heaved a long-suffering sigh and twisted away.

"Where did this silence come from, sweetheart? It's a cruel weapon," Sven stated. Tension in his voice revealed how cruel.

She gave a huffy shrug of her shoulders. Her voice might be silent, but her body was talking. Sven kept a firm hold and waited.

"Sweetheart, I aim to spank you before this day is done, but I'd rather talk first. Your behavior is damaging to our family. It can't go on nor can it happen again."

Caroline gave a more violent jerk. She would have succeeded in breaking free if Sven wasn't so determined she would not.

"All right, then. A spanking now and another when we've figured our way through. You are my wife, my responsibility, my love. It's my job to keep my family on even ground, and I aim to do it." Sven hoped for compliance, but it was not to be.

He stood her between his legs, unbuttoned her skirt, and untied the bow to her bloomers. When those garments dropped to the ground, he lifted her out of them and laid her over his left thigh. He closed his eyes and waited for the sound of her voice. Nothing.

He lifted his hand and let it fall onto her right cheek. His handprint appeared red against alabaster skin. Damn. He enjoyed seeing this sign of ownership displayed on her bottom. He spanked her left cheek and watched for the bloom of his handprint. Then he applied himself to the job of reconciliation. He spanked right, left, left, right until her bottom glowed deep pink. He moved his spanks to the tender place where the curve of her sweet bottom swept up from her thighs. With crisp upward strokes, he set her bottom on jiggling fire.

Caroline cried. Tears pooled on the floor. Her body jerked with each well-placed stroke.

"Stop, Sven. It hurts," she cried.

"I know it does, sweetheart. A spanking that didn't hurt would be no good to either of us," he replied. "Are you ready to talk to me. Really talk? We must come to an understanding."

Her delayed response brought another flurry of upward spanks. Sven added a few to her flaming cheeks to reinforce his message. He would spank until she spoke.

"Stop. I'll talk." Her voice was strangled through her tears.

Sven lifted her carefully to his lap letting her little bottom rest between his open knees. He pulled her body into his chest and rubbed her back.

"Tell me why you thought not talking was a good idea?" he demanded.

"It's what my mama did," she stated.

"Well, I didn't know that," Sven's reply was puzzled. "Did it work?"

"I suppose, but it was terrible. She wouldn't answer when you spoke to her. She'd just look like she heard a ghost," Caroline replied.

"How long did that last?"

"Sometimes a week. If I apologized and begged, she might give me a little kiss on the cheek, and I'd know it was over." Caroline twisted the material of his shirt in her little hand. "I hated it."

"Did she do this to your father?" Sven asked.

"Yes," Caroline admitted.

"What did he do?"

"Waited for it to blow over. Went to town more often. Stayed away from the house." Caroline listed her father's favored responses to her mother's cold silence.

"You hated the punishment of silence, and yet you used it on me," Sven mused.

Caroline blushed. "Well, it seemed to work for Mama."

"I don't believe it did, sweetheart. Nothing was solved. Your father avoided her, and her children disliked her. Is that about the truth of it?" Sven questioned.

Caroline gave the matter some thought. "Yes, I suppose it is."

"Do you want that kind of marriage? Do you want to drive me out of the house? Do you want our children to fear your abandonment? That's what she did, after all. She made you feel alone." Sven patted her back and rocked the chair.

"No, I don't want that," Caroline stated.

"Good, because I won't allow it. I took an oath to honor and protect you. You took one to honor and obey. We took those vows before God, and we will live up to them." Sven pushed the rocker with his right foot a few times. "Caroline, we need to talk, discuss, maybe even argue, but never ignore, never turn our backs. I know our wedding day did not go as we'd hoped." He snorted at his understatement. "I know you are angry about Lars and upset that the town witnessed our disgrace."

Caroline wiggled in his arms. "Oh, Sven," she cried, "we're ruined."

"No, we're not. We're the same people we were before Lars rode into town. We've both made mistakes, but I suspect most people have. I told Lars I'm done chasing after him. He's still lurking about San Miguel, but he hasn't approached me. He's staying in your old rooms. Before you get yourself in trouble by working up your anger, he's my brother and a soul in need of understanding. I wish I could give it to him, but he won't accept it. If he ever comes to me with an open heart, I will welcome him," Sven pushed the chair a little harder.

"All right, Sven, I understand. But what about the things he said? Can we stay here after all of that? I love San Miguel. I love John and Marcie especially, but I'm afraid. I loved Cold Spring, too, and they drove me away." She shivered in his arms.

"I have given that quite a bit of thought and prayer. First, let's wait and see. If the congregation accepts us after a little time, and the children return to school after vacation, perhaps we'll stay," Sven suggested.

"If they don't?"

"Let's cross that bridge when we get to it," Sven said. "Just so we understand each other. You will not punish me or our children with icy silence."

Caroline nodded her head.

"Words, Caroline, I need to be sure you understand."

"I understand," she declared.

"Before I finish your spanking," he began.

"Finish? Sven, no, I understand," Caroline objected.

"Before I finish your spanking," Sven began again, "I want to make a few things known. If I ever have to spank you twice for the same thing, I will use more than my hand."

"What do you mean?" Her voice held concern and a touch of panic.

"I'll never injure you, sweetheart. Did your father never spank your mother?" he enquired.

"No."

"Well, that explains quite a lot. I've been working on a little paddle, or I might use a wooden spoon or your hairbrush. It's best you learn the lesson the first time. Anyway, Caroline, no one ever died from having their bottom warmed."

"I don't want you to do that, Sven," Caroline said.

"Then don't make me, sweetheart. It's as simple as that. Don't make me." Sven paused for a brief moment. "Another thing. I decide on the punishment. The when, the where, and the how. Let's finish."

Sven lifted her from his lap and laid her over his left thigh once more. He secured her legs with his right one. That would help her lie still and avoid injury. He inspected her bottom. It was a dark pink. He wouldn't be too harsh. They had, he hoped, reached an understanding.

Lifting his right hand, he brought it down with a crisp stroke. He resumed his earlier pace. When he had counted to twenty, and Caroline lay draped over his leg and sobbing, he stopped. It was enough.

He rubbed her bright bottom and patted her back. Damn. He remembered that night by the river. The sight of her punished backside had driven reason and responsibility clear out of his mind. But she was his wife now, and, due to Caroline's hostile silence, they hadn't consummated the marriage.

He dropped his hand and wedged it between her thighs. He smiled when his bride parted her legs. It was an invitation he couldn't refuse. His fingers drifted to her center. Parting her lips, he drove a finger into her cave. When she moaned, he replaced it with two and began a rhythm.

Removing his fingers, he sought the little nub of pleasure that lay at the peak of her entrance. He rubbed and pinched and rubbed and pinched until her movement was frantic.

Sven lifted her into his arms and carried her to their bedroom. Laying her in the middle of the expanse, he unbuttoned her blouse and pulled it free. He feasted on her breasts, pulling, biting, massaging. He withdrew from his meal long enough to remove his own clothes before positioning himself between her thighs. Draping her legs over his shoulders, he supported her bottom with his large hands and lifted her to his mouth.

His tongue continued the assault until he felt the waves of her passion. Caroline's body jerked in his hands, and he laid his tongue flat and pressed. When he'd wrung every last measure from her writhing body, he laid her flat on the mattress.

"I'm going to take you now," he whispered. In a single stroke, he entered and pushed to the farthest end of the place designed especially for him. Caroline whimpered. Her hips pushed against him with insistent need. He withdrew and plunged, withdrew and plunged.

Sven pulled back and Caroline groaned. "Turn over, sweetheart." He pulled her hips up and laid a gentle hand on her shoulders until her upper body lay on the bed and her beautiful pink bottom waved an invitation. He squeezed her buttocks and patted the flaming skin. He entered her and captured her hips in his hands. Holding her steady, he brought them both to shuddering completion.

He fell to his side taking Caroline with him. She was snuggled into the curve of his body. He took one breast into his hand and sighed.

"Sleep," he ordered.

She obeyed.

# CHAPTER 13

CAROLINE

*C*aroline had lost weight since the wedding. She was a scrawny bird. Her shoulder blades poked through her dress like fragile wings. Her legs and arms were sticks, twigs really. Sven begged her to eat. He even threatened to spank her if she didn't consume the tiny portions he laid on her plate. She tried. Truly, she tried, but her throat clutched shut when she attempted to swallow and not a single morsel could pass. Sven would not spank her for this. She knew he hoped his half-hearted threat might work, but he also knew she was not being willfully disobedient. He was worried. Worried and sad.

Caroline twisted her hands in her lap. Her fingers white claws that scratched at her skirt.

She sat, as always, in the front pew on the left side of the church. The spot reserved for the reverend's wife. Caroline did not look behind her, but she felt emptiness at her back. A room once full of life and breath was near vacant. For the second Sunday in a row, the town had turned its back. The few people present shifted restlessly in their seats. The service should have begun, but their minister sat in a straight back chair staring at the floor between his boots.

Long minutes passed before he rose and surveyed the little group.

"Thank you for joining us today," he began. "I'm pleased to announce that Granny Wilkins has recovered." He gestured at an older woman in a plain brown calico dress. "Welcome back," he said.

Granny Wilkins rewarded him with a near toothless grin.

"Let us pray," Sven said. "Lord, thank you for community. Thank you for the goodness of friendship and the joy of love. Amen."

The congregation lifted their heads and glanced right and left. That prayer was mighty short and a little odd.

Sven stepped to the front of the platform. "I had a different verse in mind for today, but in my meditation, another came to me. It is Jeremiah 29:11. *"For I know the plans I have for you,"* declares the Lord, *"plans to prosper you and not to harm you, plans to give you hope and a future."*

Caroline slipped to the front of the bench. Her bottom poised on the edge. Her emotions raced from joy to despair and made a few stops in between as she observed her husband. Poor Sven. He'd lost weight, too, she realized. Being so big, it took longer before the change was noticeable. His beautiful pale eyes were bruised. She scolded herself. What kind of a wife was she? A wife, especially a minister's wife, should be a helpmeet. Why, she was nothing but a burden to the sad, sorrowful man. She held her breath. The prickling in her stomach warned her of, well, she didn't rightly know. Her husband rose and moved to the center of the platform. His eyes scanned the half-empty church and hovered for long moments on her face. Caroline flinched at the sound of his scratchy, rough voice.

"I have disappointed this community that I love so much. I

never intended to deceive or lead through misapprehension, but by withholding facts from my past, I did. I convinced myself that it did not matter, but it did." A sharp inhale of surprise swept the church.

"My brother put matters to rights. He informed the town of facts you had every right to know. I was not involved in the actual robbery of the bank, but I was wrong not to intervene. I only thought of my brother and not the injury to the community who trusted their bank. Far worse, I injured my wife whom I love more than the breath in my body. I left her alone to face the indignation and condemnation of the little town where we grew up. Left her alone to face humiliation and scorn for anticipating our vows. We have been led back to one another and blessed with a son. I will forever weep for the travail that Caroline endured alone, but I will go down on my knees every day and thank the Lord for bringing Caroline and Micah back into my life." He shrugged his shoulders. "I am resigning as your minister, but nothing need change between us. I am here. I am available. I will still rejoice in your triumphs and help shoulder your burdens. I always have time, and time to spare, for friends. I am here." The congregation sat motionless, suspended in mutual unhappiness. "I am here," he repeated.

Caroline met his wan smile with one of her own.

"The Lord promises plans to prosper and not hurt. Plans of hope and plans for a bright future. I trust in those plans." He ran a weary hand across his face. "Caroline and I will decide, with God's help, on our next steps. Steps made together and with faith. Thank you."

He stepped down and offered her his hand. Caroline seized it like a swimmer going under for the third time, and they walked down the aisle and out the door. Loki rose from his favorite spot at the back and followed. The congregation watched them leave with open mouths and not a few tears.

"Are you sure, Sven?" Caroline enquired. She reached down and ran her fingers through Loki's rough fur.

"I am," he replied. "I feel like a burden has been lifted." He draped an arm over her small shoulders and pulled her close to his side. "Because of me this church has become a house divided. It's the best thing, for us and for the congregation." He brushed a kiss across her temple. "I'd like Micah to stay with me a few days every week when school starts up again. He enjoys playing with Katie, so I wouldn't deny him the pleasure completely, but I have time to make up with the little man." She squeezed his hand in agreement.

"I've got some carpentry jobs lined up. I'll check with the customers to be sure the items are still wanted. We should talk about those plans I mentioned. We can stay; we can go. But whatever path we choose, we walk it together." He turned her to face him and held her thin shoulders in his hands. "Let's get Micah. I'd like to take my wife and son out to dinner at the café." He dropped a wink and a smile that throbbed all the way to her toes before settling heavy and hot in her abdomen.

"Why Mr. Nielson, that is an excellent idea," Caroline acknowledged. She looped her hand through his elbow and held on tight.

When they emerged with Micah bundled against the cold, Caroline tipped her head at the man across the dusty street.

"I see him, sweetheart," Sven said.

Lars slouched against the front of the Mercantile. The store was closed. The owner and his wife being among the townspeople who refused Sven's ministry and no longer hosted the Fellowship Hour after the service. Fellowship Hour, she snorted. Their recipe for fellowship was mighty skimpy.

Lars' hat was pulled low over his eyes. His legs were crossed at the ankle. Caroline chuckled. You'd think it was a summer day, and he was passing a pleasant afternoon instead of bone chilling January. Sven gave a nod, and she couldn't be completely sure, but she was fairly certain his hat took a little dip.

Caroline smiled at her husband. She was hungry. Why, she planned to order fried chicken with all the fixings. If she had even a speck of room left, she'd have cherry pie. The café made a wonderful cherry pie. She was a little jealous if truth be told. Her pie was never as flakey or fine. Although Sven, bless his heart, ate with gusto and declared it the best he'd ever had.

Caroline guided the last bit of pie to her mouth, swallowed and laid her fork on the empty plate. She rubbed her stomach. "I am so full," she groaned.

"I loved seeing you eat, sweetheart," Sven said as he pushed his chair from the table. "I've been worried."

"Micah needs his nap." She scooped the boy into her arms. "Let's go home."

That morning they had been pensive, nervous, and uncomfortable with each other and with the town. Uncertain of the route their lives should follow. The air had cleared. Caroline took deep, unfettered breaths. She lowered the child into his crib. When she turned, she ran into a wall of muscle. Raising her head, she met her husband's hot gaze.

"Sven?" His name a question.

His answer was a kiss, one hand cupping her bottom while the other pulled her pelvis into the hardness of his need.

"I want you, sweetheart," he whispered into her ear.

Caroline nodded and snuggled her head into her husband's chest. His hands went to work at the buttons on the back of her dress. Before they were through the door to their own room, he'd pulled it over her head, tossed it away, and went to work at the laces of her stays.

"Why do you wear these? You're so small. Do you really need them?" He frowned at the red marks left on her pale skin.

Caroline cast a baleful glance at her bosom. She had hoped for more. She shrugged her shoulders. "Are they enough? I heard men like big breasts, but…"

"You're perfect. Don't wear them again. They hurt you, and I won't allow it." He lowered his head to her rose-brown nipple and pulled it into his mouth. Her back arched and offered her breast for his pleasure. His mouth never left its work while he placed her on the bed.

Sven took both her hands in one of his and lifted them over her head. "Leave them here," he ordered. Caroline sighed. She loved his dominance, his masculinity. She placed her body in his hands with joy and greedy anticipation.

She lowered her right hand and slid it down his back to the curve of his buttocks.

Sven lifted his head and regarded her with eyebrows furrowed. "Caroline?" he grumbled before returning her hand above her head. "Arms up. Don't make me say it again."

Caroline quivered. Sven returned his attention to her breasts before kissing his way down her stomach. He separated her thighs and kissed the sensitive skin at the inside of each leg. Caroline struggled. Every sinew in her body urged her to plunge her hands into his hair and hold on tight, but she had her instructions.

A long finger stroked her front to back before snaking its way into her body. Her breath froze in her throat, and her hips thrust toward the ceiling. Sven emitted an approving growl before adding a second finger to his exploration.

She climbed higher, trembling, reaching toward the top. Her head thrashed from side to side. Her arm flew down and seized his buttock, pulling him, prodding him to enter.

His hands were warm on her hips as he flipped her body. The spank that followed was delicious heat. She lifted her hips towards him. Invitation delivered.

"Caroline, hands up," Sven repeated his command before delivering two, three, four more spanks to her wriggling bottom.

She obeyed. The next spanks were light, playful, full of sting but not bite.

Her hips left the bed as Sven pulled her bottom high and spread her legs with his massive thigh. He nudged her open and pressed into her waiting cave with one small thrust, withdrew, ventured deeper, withdrew, plunged hard and deep, harder, deeper, faster, longer.

Caroline exploded, quivered, found release.

Carried in Sven's arms as he fell to the bed, they lay glistening with sweat, breathless, on a Sunday afternoon following church. Caroline giggled.

"What?" Her husband turned on his side and pulled her closer to his sheltering frame.

"At home we read quietly on Sunday afternoons. No playing allowed." She stroked the soft hair that covered his chest. "This is much more fun."

"If the Lord didn't want a husband and wife to enjoy their love, he wouldn't have made it so damn marvelous." He nuzzled her neck and placed a series of tiny kisses behind her ear.

"Sven," she scolded, "you swore."

"Sometimes nothing else will do," he stated. "But don't you try it," he warned. "Now, wife, let's take a nap before our little man wakes up."

Caroline's eyes drifted shut. She was already there.

## CHAPTER 14

SVEN

Sven slowly surveyed his wife's sweet bottom. He was sorry to bring her pain, but, damn, if he didn't love the view. Caroline turned her head with an unspoken question in her eyes. He shook his head. "No, we're not done." He gave her buttocks a series of swift spanks before kneading the inflamed skin.

"Now, sweetheart, what were you thinking? I told you before not to go to the MacGregor farm without me. The man is a loose cannon." Anger vibrated through his voice like a swirling wind.

"I thought since he had become our friend – you know, sending his boys to school and coming to church – I thought, I thought your opinion would have changed," she said as she peeked at him over her shoulder.

"But you didn't ask me."

Caroline shook her head. "I'm sorry."

"Did he shoot that damn rifle at you?" he growled.

She hesitated.

"Caroline?" The question was punctuated with a hearty smack.

"Yes." She gave her head a frantic shake. "Over my head. He didn't shoot at me, and when the boys begged him to put the rifle down, he did."

Sven closed his eyes. The grinding of his teeth echoed in his head. "The man shot at my wife. Caroline, I can't lose you. MacGregor is a lonely, angry man. He drinks. That old rifle could go off at any time and in any direction." He swallowed hard. "Please, please, you must obey me when it involves your safety. I can't quite figure it. Why did you go to the MacGregor farm when you know I forbid it?"

His wife shifted over his thighs, and he moaned. He wanted her something fierce, but the punishment wasn't at an end.

"You were hard at work on the table you're making for the Kemps. I didn't want to disturb you." She tried that excuse on for size. It didn't fit.

"You and Micah always come first. You know that. If it was that important, I would drive you there myself. You know that," he repeated his chorus.

He felt his wife draw a long breath. "I get tired of obeying you. I like to make some decisions on my own, and I decided to pay a visit to two of my favorite students." Her sassy response irritated like fingernails on a chalkboard.

Sven laid half dozen crisp swats to her crimson backside. "I do not tell you who to befriend, what to buy, what to cook, what opinions to hold or how to care for our son. You make decisions all the live long day." He added another round of spanks for good measure. "But when it comes to the safety of our family, I make the decisions. That was true in Minnesota, it's true today, and it will be true tomorrow and the day after that until they carry me feet first out the door. The sooner you understand that, the better it will be for your behind."

Caroline wailed, "I'm sorry. I won't do it again."

"You'd best not, sweetheart." He reached behind him to fetch the wooden spoon he had laid out for this final purpose. "This is the second time I've had to spank you for going alone to the MacGregor place. I told you before that if I had to punish you twice for the same thing, I would use more than my hand." He placed the spoon in Caroline's line of vision.

"No, Sven, please," his wife begged. His heart clenched in his chest, but he was a man of his word. "Give me your hands." He held them behind her back. "I don't want to strike your hands. Only your bottom."

He tapped her right cheek twice before delivering a sharp crack with the spoon. He repeated the pattern, tap-tap-spank, tap-tap-spank, tap-tap-spank. His wife squirmed and twisted in an unsuccessful escape attempt. He waited for her to settle before completing his task, lifting her into his arms, and snuggling her against his chest.

When her crying ceased, he carried her to their room and tucked her into bed. "Rest, sweetheart." He tiptoed to the door and turned back for a last look. She was already asleep. He grinned before closing the door with a careful click.

He fed Micah dinner and bathed him in a large pan in the kitchen. Loki fetched a ball that Micah threw with crazy abandon until Sven put him to bed, and Caroline slept through it all. When he climbed into bed, he pulled her close to his body but was careful not to wake her. Sven wanted her to rest. She must have been powerful tired.

The next morning Sven patted Caroline's back and smoothed the black hair from her face. "Sweetheart, wake up." He kissed her neck, her forehead, behind her ear.

"What time is it?" she mumbled.

"Seven in the morning," he chuckled. "You slept through dinner and all through the night."

"Oh, Micah." Caroline lurched to a sit.

"Micah's fine. We had dinner, and he went to bed. I let Loki sleep in his room, which he loved. I hope I didn't start a bad habit, but what could it hurt? Having a dog for a friend is mighty fine."

His hand floated down her back and came to rest on her bottom. "Are you all right?"

"Yes, but I don't want to talk about it," she snapped. "I'm sorry. It's embarrassing."

"Spanking is a private matter and stays in our home. Anyway, between you and me there need not be embarrassment. I'm your husband," he declared. "I've seen wives spanked in public," he mused. "Maybe it was a matter that just couldn't wait." He gave her bottom a gentle swat. "Time to get up. It's Sunday, and we need to get ready for church."

"What? There's no minister," Caroline protested.

"True. But even if no one joins us, we need to spend an hour giving thanks." He rose from the bed. "I'll get Micah dressed if you rustle up some breakfast."

Thirty minutes later, Sven hustled his family out the door. They were running late, but, without a minister, he didn't figure it would matter. They would start getting ready earlier next week. Having a young one made keeping to a schedule a particular problem.

Sven bundled Micah into a quilt and waited while his wife secured her cloak. He held the baby in one arm and took possession of Caroline's arm with his other hand. The walkway was icy until the sun had a chance to throw a few bedraggled rays their way, and he didn't want her to fall.

As they approached the church, they heard a man's voice rise and fall and rise again. Sven pulled Caroline to a stop, "Let's listen for minute. We don't want to interrupt if a sermon is under way."

"Who would be preaching?" Caroline wondered.

Moving closer to the door, Sven strained to hear. "It's John Wayne," he whispered.

"Well, I see most all of the sheep have returned to the fold," John said. Disgust soaked his every word. "Since we're short one preacher, I believe I'll have my say." Boots thumped up the aisle and climbed two steps as John mounted the little platform that served as an altar.

Micah had a firm grasp of the hair on both sides of Caroline's face, and he lunged toward her planting sloppy, open mouthed kisses on his mama's face. Sven choked back a laugh and placed a finger on his lips. Caroline nodded and moved away from the door. Micah and silence were not a comfortable pair.

John continued, "Sven always picked a verse and shared his thoughts. It was a preaching style I was particularly fond of. Never been a man to cotton to scolding, anger or righteous proclamations." Sven leaned closer. "Since his brother busted up the wedding and some fine citizens of our town turned their backs on our preacher, I've pondered a verse or two myself."

"I don't take much to scolding either, Mr. Wayne, if that's what you have in mind." The woman's tone was insulted arrogance. Skirts rustled.

"Sit back down, Mrs. Peterson. You can have your say when I'm done if you're so inclined," John said.

Another voice added, "Sit down, Elvira. I done let you take the bit in your mouth once too often." More rustling followed by suspenseful silence.

"The first verse is found in Genesis. Wouldn't you know it. Right away two brothers are fighting, jealous, riled up. I had a couple brothers myself, and I'm not proud to say it, but we came to blows more than once. Why, if my ma hadn't stepped in and taken a strap to us now and again, we might have killed each other. I love those scamps now, but brothers have their own kind of growing up to do." The low chuckle of male recognition swept the room. "Sven's brother brought trouble to his door. He busted into this very room on what should have been one of the happiest days of Sven's life and ripped it to shreds, laid waste to all the good Sven has done for our town with his mean words. Was Lars jealous or just a low-down snake? I don't have the answer to that question, but Sven's sin was trying to keep his brother from harm. Now, maybe he should have done different. Maybe he should have turned him over to the law right away."

Sven hung on every word. Those questions had kept him up many a night.

"We all know the story of Cain and Abel. Cain really does kill his brother. Where was his ma that day? The Bible doesn't say, but no ma can watch her children every minute." This time the laughter was feminine. "Cain is jealous, so jealous he takes Abel's life. When the Lord calls him to account, the only defense he can come up with is a question: Am I my brother's keeper? That's a mighty famous question, and I think we all know God's answer. *Hell, yes, you are your brother's keeper. You stand together or you fall together."*

John paused for a moment. "Sven was caught in that old dilemma. Was he his brother's keeper? He thought he was. It was bred in his bones."

Sven watched as Caroline set Micah down on his feet to practice walking. Loki trotted beside, giving the boy's face an occasional lick.

"Enough about Sven. I'm curious about all of you. Have you ever made a mistake? Done something you aren't proud of? Said something you regret? Does anyone in this room dare to say they have led a blameless life?" John waited. "I didn't think so. John chapter eight, verse one wraps this one up tight. It says, *"He that is without sin among you, let him cast the first stone".* I'd say there have been plenty of stones thrown in this town lately. Too many."

A petulant female voice broke in. "Mr. Wayne," she began.

"You'll have your turn, Mrs. Peterson. I'm almost done." John cleared his throat. "I saved the biggest gun for last. The second Commandment tells us to love our neighbor as ourselves. The second of ten rules given to us by God himself. Love they neighbor as thyself. Now, Sven made mistakes, but he's a good man, a man I'm honored to count as friend. I'm sorry to say that I'm a little ashamed of our town, and its inability to forgive. That's all I got to say."

John's boots sounded on the two steps.

A shrill female voice scalded the air. "There are other rules in the Bible, Mr. Wayne. Rules about fornication. Rules about truth. Rules about honesty. You brought that man to our town. It's no wonder you defend him."

Sven stepped back as the door flew open and Elvira Peterson stormed out. Her nose tilted to the sky. Her boots beating a quick tattoo. Her husband followed in her wake. "I'm sorry, Sven. It's been easier to let her fume and fuss than to take her in hand. I feel responsible for her gossip and uncharitable actions. I intend to call her to account, but I'm afraid the damage is done." He followed his wife with purposeful steps.

John emerged and laid a hand on Sven's shoulder. "Sometimes I miss the old days when men outnumbered women ten to one."

"I thank you for your words this morning, friend," Sven said. "We'll just have to wait a bit and see if they were taken to heart."

The two men watched as Elvira Peterson pranced up the street kicking a dust cloud of self-righteous fury in her wake.

"Yup," John sighed. "I miss those days."

# CHAPTER 15

SVEN

"*L*et's go greet your mama, little man." Sven snatched his son up as he toddled past and swooped him over his head and around in a circle before settling him on his arm.

"Mo," Micah shrieked and bounced his bottom up and down in the signal for renewed flight.

"Maybe later, son. We need to say howdy to our woman first." Sven's large hand patted the small back.

A sigh signaled the tot's displeasure, but he laid his head on his father's shoulder and popped a damp thumb into his mouth.

Sven closed the door to his workshop and carried his son into the house. He stirred the soup simmering on the black cast iron stove before sitting in the large rocker with Micah on his knee.

Light footsteps pattered up the stairs and paused before the door opened enough to let Caroline's slim body slip into the room.

As soon as he laid eyes on her drooping shoulders, pale face and trembling hands he knew. "No better, darling?" A rhetorical question, her body told all.

"No. No, they're not coming back," Caroline answered. "We'd best face facts. Mrs. Peterson and her band of biddies has won." Color flamed in two spots of hectic red on her cheeks. "And Lars." She stamped her foot. "Lars is still hanging about watching us come and go. Why doesn't he move on? I suppose he wants to gloat. I can just hear him. *Look at me. I managed to ruin my brother's life in San Miguel. Let him build a house, a life, a reputation, and I'll knock it down.* Oh, I hate him. I hate them both." Tears rolled unchecked down her white face and landed on her small bosom.

"Caroline," he scolded. "Surely you don't mean that. Mrs. Peterson is an unforgiving woman, and I suspect not a happy one." He cleared his throat. "Lars, well, Lars might have done what he set out to do, but causing us heartache hasn't made him happy. He's a sad, lonely man. We should pray for them both."

Caroline wrapped her arms around her middle and glared. "Sometimes, Sven, I want to punch you. You are too good, too generous. I plan to be mad at them for a long while." She stamped across the room and hung her cloak on a peg.

Sven set Micah on his feet and watched as he toddled towards their Husky. Loki would keep the boy out of trouble. He gathered his wife into his arms and pulled her onto his lap. "Tell me," the command was harsh, but his voice was a gentle breeze.

"The same students came again today. The MacGregor boys, Adam and Ava Wayne, Tommy, Jeanette and Joe Thornton and little Lillian Grey. She's only five, but the older children watch out for her." He had heard this litany before. After every school day for the past two weeks, in fact. What lay behind her fury today?

The only sounds were Micah's thumping pats on the big dog's side and the gentle squeak of the rocking chair. Sven waited.

"Marcie Wayne came to fetch the children after school. The mothers of the other twelve students are taking turns holding lessons. She didn't want me to hear of it through some nasty gossip. She's a good friend," Caroline sniffled.

Sven pulled a handkerchief from his pocket and mopped his

bride's face. He put the cloth to her nose. "Blow," he commanded. Caroline shook her head and attempted to push his big hand away. "You're as bad as Micah. Blow," he repeated. When she had obeyed, he pulled her close to his chest and took up waiting again. Two weeks had passed since school resumed after Christmas vacation. The seven students returned to school. The other twelve remained absent. Why all the tears today?

He settled his wife against his chest and pushed the floor with his big foot. Resting his chin on the top of her head, he closed his eyes and resumed his vigil. She would tell him when she was ready, but they wouldn't leave the chair until he knew the source of her upset.

Time ticked by. Micah lay with his nose pressed to Loki's and proceeded to speak with the dog in their secret language. Loki's tail thumped a steady rhythm on the floor. The fire in the stove popped. The rocker squeaked. Sven waited.

A shudder wracked through his wife's body, and fresh tears splashed his arm.

"Little Lillian," Caroline managed to speak around gulps of grief. "Little Lillian asked me a question today."

"Oh?" Sven prompted. "And what was it? Full of questions, she is. A curious little scamp."

"She asked," Caroline fought to control her voice. "She asked what a b...b...bastard is. I asked where she had heard that word. Well, it seems two ladies with very mean faces came to visit her ma. Her ma offered tea, but they refused."

Sven brought the chair to a halt. "And then?"

"Then the two mean ladies told her ma that she shouldn't let Lillian go to school when the teacher is no better than a harlot. They said Mrs. Nielson's baby was a bastard no matter that she was married now, and no matter what John Wayne had to say." Caroline shivered and buried her face in his shirt.

"What did you tell Lillian?" Sven asked.

"I told her to ask her mother," Caroline replied. "She said she had, but her mother said they would discuss it when she was older. I said Lillian had to listen to her ma and wait until she was ready for grown-up words. That seemed to satisfy her, and she went off to play with Ava and Jeanette."

"If I were Elvira Peterson's husband, I'd spank her every day for a month for the trouble she's caused. Mean-spirited harpy," Sven exclaimed.

Caroline laughed. "What happened to poor, unhappy Mrs. Peterson who deserves our sympathy?"

Sven smiled down at his pretty wife. Her laughter was a balm to his spirit. "Well, I do believe she is unhappy. Partly because her husband doesn't care enough to keep her in line. She needs a spanking. It would calm her down and make her feel loved. That's why I pity her, Caroline. She doesn't feel safe, loved, cared for. If I was still his minister, I would counsel him to take her directly to the woodshed and be damn sure she was properly punished, loved, and reassured."

Sven and Caroline watched as Micah rose to a wobbly stand, took two steps, and fell to his padded bottom. He crawled to a chair and pulled himself upright again before beaming a four-tooth grin. His parents clapped their hands at his daring.

Caroline turned to face her husband and laced her fingers with his. "Oh, Sven, this was hard to hear, but it got me thinking. How many people in town are saying just what Lillian heard? I can't bear the thought that when Micah is older, someone, an old biddy like Elvira Peterson or maybe even another child who doesn't know the meaning of the word, will call our son a b...b... I can't even bring myself to say it. If we stay, it will happen." She paused. "We have to leave. We need to go where no one knows us. You could preach again..."

"No, I'm done with that. All my life in Cold Spring, it was expected of me, so I expected it of myself. No, I want to be a husband, friend, father, and brother, if Lars will let me. I'll be a carpenter, too. I can support us that way, but not a preacher."

Sven shook his head. "Not a preacher. I don't feel that calling anymore."

"As long as we're together, I'm happy." She squeezed his hand. "I think I'll teach until the end of the month. I won't accept money when most of the children aren't attending school. Anyway, little Lillian's story today made me see something else. The school has become a battleground divided between those who support us and those who don't. I won't be the cause of bad feelings. Bad feelings that could take years to heal."

"I agree, sweetheart. The school board wasn't happy about a married teacher anyway. John Wayne talked them into letting you continue," Sven replied. "We'll wait until good weather, and then we'll leave San Miguel. Gives us a while to figure out where we want to go." They rocked in quiet for a few minutes. "I can go to the school board and tell them you resign as of the end of January if you want me to. It's the right thing. We both came to San Miguel hoping to make it a better place. We sure as shooting don't want to make it worse."

"Thank you, Sven. If you really don't mind, I'd just as soon not see the school board." She shrugged her tiny shoulders. "I wanted to be a good teacher. I tried so hard. I'm afraid I might either cry or yell, and neither one would be helpful. I'll tell the students tomorrow that I will teach two more weeks."

Sven lifted his wife to the ground. "You change Micah, and I'll ladle up the soup."

They paused for a long, hard hug. Decisions made. Choices considered. Paths selected. Sven released a long-held sigh before patting his wife's back. "We'll be all right, sweetheart," he reassured. "We surely will."

Days passed as days do, sunrise to sunset. Two other facts as reliable as the rotation around the sun were that it was the coldest winter in memory, and Lars would be standing across the street with feet crossed and hat pulled low watching them come and go. Oh, and the third was that it required all his restraint and self-control to wait until Micah was asleep before he took his wife to bed and demonstrated his love for her. He spent his days building, sanding, caring for Micah and planning all the ways he could pleasure her. He longed to bring her to shuddering, shattering climaxes, watch her fall apart beneath his hands, hear her call his name. He shook his head. Lord have mercy, if he died tomorrow, he'd had a peek at paradise right here on earth. Good thing he'd given up preaching. He was pretty sure some blasphemy lay in those thoughts.

He couldn't do much about the cold except keep the wood box at home and school full and wrap his wife and son in scarves and blankets to keep the sharp, piercing wind at bay.

As for Lars, he was a mystery. Sven had expected him to leave town and wreak havoc elsewhere, but he remained standing and staring. When his brother decided to talk, he'd be ready to listen.

A rush of frigid air shocked the room as Caroline slipped in the door. Sven pulled her into his arms for a scorching kiss before unwinding layers of scarves from around her soft, tempting neck.

"How was school?" he asked between nibbling her ear and pressing her closer.

"Good. We're working on a few projects. Maps, battle diagrams, timelines, artwork all focused on the Revolutionary War. Each child will have something to take home on the last day to show their parents." Caroline gave a rueful chuckle. "I'm taking the easy way out. Normally we would be looking at causes and outcomes of the Civil War at this time of year. Sentiment still runs high around that topic, though, so I decided to go out with something less controversial, coward that I am."

"Wise, sweetheart, not cowardly. I reckon we've stirred up enough controversy in this town already." His kisses descended to that sweet place where her neck met her shoulder. His hands cradled her bosom while his thumbs whispered across her nipples.

"Something smells good," Caroline sniffed at the air.

"I have stew simmering. I aim to keep you and Micah full of hot food to chase the cold away." Sven slid a hand over her bottom and pulled her tight to his body.

"Oki," a sleepy voice shouted. The big dog stretched and yawned before trotting into the baby's room.

Sven tapped Caroline's rounded backside. "Somebody's awake, sweetheart. But I've got big plans for later."

He released her and called, "Where's Micah?" The game was on.

Like bashful kisses, a hint of warmth blew into town the following day. Sven stood on the porch with Micah wrapped in a single blanket and waited for Caroline to get home from school. He tipped his head in a small salute to his brother across the street. A return nod and a shift in stance was the reply. Darned if he knew what the man was doing, wanted or planned. Sven sighed before turning his eyes up the street.

At the sight of Caroline turning the corner, he heaved Micah onto his shoulders and strode to meet her.

"How was your day, sweetheart?" He laid a kiss on her warm cheek.

"Good. Great, even. The children were able to play outside, and we had such fun. Duck, duck goose, jumping rope, tag. I let them have extra time since we've been cooped up all week."

Caroline's eyes brimmed with unshed tears. "I am going to miss them. Only three more days. I thought I'd bake cookies for the last day. We'll end on a sweet note."

Sven dropped his arm around her small shoulders and tucked her into his side. "The children will love that. I don't guess the MacGregor boys get much in the way of treats." They walked in silence, sweet and content. Micah clutched at his father's hair, kicked his feet, and babbled.

Caroline peered up at the child towering over her on his father's shoulders. "Mama," she said and patted her chest.

"Oki," Micah shouted before dissolving into giggles and energetic hair pulling.

"He's funnin' you. If you ignore it, he'll be saying your name day and night. In fact, once he commences with 'mama this' and 'mama that' you'll wonder that you ever wanted to hear it."

"I suppose you're right," Caroline conceded. "I wonder where he got that stubborn streak." She speared her husband with a pointed look.

Sven lifted Micah from his shoulders and settled him in his wife's arms. "Take Micah, and get him down for his nap," he instructed as he opened the door to their home. "I'm going back out to the school and fill the wood box."

"There's no need, Sven," Caroline placed a hand on his arm and tugged him inside. "I only used a little wood today. The box is at least half full." She turned so that the baby rested between their two bodies, but she'd managed to insert her thigh between his legs.

Mercy! This woman burned like a brand. She left a trail of heat wherever she touched, and the gentle pressure on his manhood was raising possibilities. He stroked his hand over her buttocks and pulled her close so she could feel the hard truth.

Caroline's deep blue eyes were clouded with desire, and her little pink tongue darted out between her petal soft lips. It was an invitation he wouldn't turn down. He could take Micah with him tomorrow at lunch and check on the school's wood box. He had a different fire to tend right here in his house.

He scooped Micah under one arm and turned Caroline toward their bedroom door. He landed a hearty swat on her bottom. "You need a nap, sweetheart. Go get in bed. I'll be in to join you as soon as Micah is settled." A protest began to form behind her eyes. She balked at orders, and he didn't issue many. But, hell's bells, she'd kindled the spark. "No arguments. Go." Another swift spank had her scurrying for the door.

"Time for Micah's nap," Sven said. The child yawned and rubbed at sleepy eyes.

"Oki?" he asked.

"Yes, Loki can sleep with you." Sven snapped his fingers, and the big dog stretched with two front paws on the floor and his behind waving in the air before following the pair into the baby's room.

"Sleep tight," Sven closed the door and turned determined steps toward the room he shared with Caroline. His wife was a bundle of contradictions, and he loved it. She might be waiting placid as one of the big lakes back home on a sweet summer night, or she might be flitting about the room doing a chore or two, disobeying his orders to be ready for a nap. He swung the door open.

"Caroline," he growled, "I told you to be in bed. What are you doing?"

"This drawer needed seeing to, Sven. It's a jumble," Caroline offered.

"I'll show you what needs seeing too, and it's not that drawer." This was the game she'd chosen to play, and he was more than happy to oblige... more than happy.

He pulled her between his legs. "Look at me, Caroline." He waited until her flighty gaze met his steady one. "What did I tell you to do?"

"But–" she began.

"No buts," he interrupted. "You were to get ready for a nap, and I planned to join you. Now, we'll still get that nap, but I guess I need to remind you who wears the pants in this house."

Caroline plucked at the material covering Sven's muscular thigh. "I know who wears the pants," she scoffed.

"Good girl. Take off your skirt, and drop your bloomers while you're at it," Sven ordered.

She looked around the room. Damn. She was cute.

"Now," he reminded.

With the skirt and bloomers around her ankles, he picked her up and laid her gently across his thighs. She clenched and unclenched her little bottom. He laughed before rubbing circles on her adorable cheeks. Spank. His hand left a light pink outline. Spank. He matched it on the other side before rubbing her pale flesh again.

Caroline wiggled an invitation. Sven accepted and laid another set of moderate swats on her bottom. This was not about punishment. It was about play, a little rough perhaps, but play.

Sven spanked until she glowed light red. His hand drifted between her thighs and found the sweetest spot, damp and aching for him. He parted her legs and let a long finger find its way into the moist cave. Caroline groaned and pressed her bottom off his thighs and into his hand.

A second finger joined the invasion. He pressed them in, pulled them out, pressed them in before finding the source of her pleasure and circling the nub. He returned with his two-fingered assault, but let his thumb massage until she squirmed in need.

Lifting her and laying her on their bed, he lowered his head to her nipples. He pulled one into his mouth through the thin material of her shift and blouse. He'd not allowed her to wear a corset since the day he'd spotted stripes of inflamed skin left by the boning. He liked it better this way. Fewer garments between him and her sweet flesh.

He removed her blouse and pulled her shift over her head before discarding his own clothes in a jumble on the floor. Draping her legs over his broad shoulders he feasted on the pink flower of her sex – first with his eyes, and then with his mouth.

"Put your arms over your head and hold on, sweetheart. I aim to take you for a ride." As her hands latched onto the bed, Sven drove into her body until he felt the end of her tunnel. He pulled back and surged forward again, again, again, again.

He pried her fingers from the bed rail, lifted her in the air, and dropped onto his back. Setting her astride his body, he lowered her slowly onto his shaft. Lifting and lowering her body, he helped her set the pace.

"Oh, hell," he whispered. "Let's try one more." He set her on the bed. "Turn over, Caroline. Get on your hands and knees." He helped his lust addled wife into position.

Sven considered. She was so tiny. A flighty bird to his bear. He lifted her hips until they achieved the perfect height, and then he held her still as he plunged, plunged and they plummeted into the abyss at the same moment Caroline called his name. Her body clutched and clasped in her completion. Damn, he loved this woman. Damn!

They lay entwined in a cocoon of cooling heat until Micah called them back to the land of responsibilities. A quick dinner, a bath for the boy, and sleep, sleep, blessed sleep.

The following morning dawned bright and warm. Unseasonably warm, but after the bitter, biting cold the heat felt like a benediction, a blessing from above.

Sven swung Micah to his shoulder and walked his pretty wife to the corner where she turned toward the Wayne place. She'd replaced her boots with light slippers, and her heavy coat for a bright blue shawl. He laughed as she nearly skipped down the dirt road in her delight.

As he returned to their house, folks smiled, nodded, called out a hearty hello. Why, you'd think he wasn't the town pariah. He tipped his hat to Lars before disappearing into his workroom.

He played with Micah for a bit before turning his attention to the table he'd nearly finished. Giving Micah a cloth so he could 'help', the two Nielson men were deeply drawn into their task when the room went dark.

"Now that's strange, Micah. Where did our light go?" he asked the busy boy.

He gathered his son into his arms and hurried to the walk. The sun had disappeared behind a huge, rolling cloud of gray that moved like a giant from a Norwegian tale toward the cowering town. Sven shivered. The temperature had dropped and showed no signs of stopping. He pulled his son close to his chest. The image of Caroline skipping down the street in her summer dress flashed across his mind. He groaned. It was followed by one of a half-full wood box. The wood box he should have filled last night. He moaned. Instead of chopping wood, he had let lust lead him. He closed his eyes.

When he opened them, Lars stood by his side. He motioned toward the roiling mass. "What do you think, brother?"

"It doesn't look exactly like snow, but it's something close," Sven replied. "Caroline is at the school with seven children and a near empty wood box. I have to get to her."

Lars nodded swift agreement. "Let me help. We know cold, and we have Loki."

Both men looked down at the muscular gray dog panting by their sides. Loki knew snow and cold. Why, many a time a Husky had pulled a sled through blinding snow with the driver lost, shivering, sometimes unconscious. If it came to a white-out, Loki could lead them, but Sven wanted more preparation, more safety.

"We'll get as much rope from the Mercantile as they have. John Wayne will have more. We can string a rope from their house to the school. It's the closest point, and two of the children with Caroline belong to him," Sven said.

Lars nodded. In the cold Wisconsin winter, a rope was strung from house to barn and from house to outhouse from the first freeze to spring. A person could get turned around in a world of white and not be found until the thaw.

"I'm going to wrap Micah in a quilt." Sven hurried into the house and returned with the boy wrapped tight.

"Mama," Micah whined. With the intuition of the young, he sensed his father's unease.

"Now you say it." Sven frowned. "You repeat that when you see her, young man."

"Martin," Sven called as he entered the Mercantile. "Seven children and my wife are soon to be stranded by the storm that's rolling in. I need all the rope you've got. Lars and I are going after them."

"That's a mighty big storm, Sven. I believe they should wait it out. You can fetch 'em after it blows over." Several men gathered around the stove nodded in agreement.

"I can't. The morning was so warm she didn't dress for this weather, and probably the children didn't either. The wood box isn't full. I'm afraid they'll freeze. Seems to be getting colder by the minute." Sven pulled his eyebrows into a ferocious glare.

"We're not from around these parts," Lars added. "Is it snow?"

"Ice," the men muttered as one.

"Ice?" Sven repeated the word like a demented parrot.

"Ice," they confirmed.

"Get me the damn rope," Sven demanded.

"Hold your horses. I'll get it." The storekeeper rushed toward the back of the room.

Sven and Lars looped the rope over their arms and strode toward the Wayne house. Loki loped beside with ears up and nose twitching. Micah burrowed into the comfort of his father's chest.

"John," Sven called as soon as they entered the Wayne's yard.

"I'm here, Sven." He stepped to the front of the porch. "I've been worrying on that storm headed our way. An ice storm is a fierce beast, and that's a monster blowing our way."

"Lars and I are headed for the schoolhouse. The temperature has dropped dangerously, and the wood box wasn't full." Sven planted his hands on his hips and glared at the ground. "I should have filled it last night, but the day had been so warm. I figured…" He let his sentence die as the first flurry of ice sliced through the air. "Sweet Jesus," he muttered.

"I was just getting ready to try on my own. Adam and Ava are out there," John said.

They joined John under the protection of the porch.

Sven dropped the rope to the floor and turned Micah into the shelter of his body. "In a Wisconsin snowstorm, we tie a rope to the house and feed it out. If we don't reach what we were aiming for, at least you can find the way back. We got all the rope the Mercantile had, and if you have any, it would help."

"And," Lars continued, "we've got Loki. Huskies know about blizzards. Now, I know this isn't snow, but the lack of vision is the same. His sense of direction beats that of any man I know. He'll lead us to them." He added his rope to the pile and secured one end to the post of John's porch.

"Give me a minute." John pulled the collar of his coat up around his throat and dashed through the pelting ice toward his barn. He returned with arms full of rope. He opened the door to his house and shouted, "Marcie, we're going for the children. Come get Micah."

Marcie shut the door behind her. "I knew you would go, so I put together bundles of all the warm clothes and shoes I could find. Tom and Amanda's kids aren't there today, so it will be the MacGregor boys, our twins, and little Lillian. I put in warm underclothes and a heavy shawl for Caroline, and she'll need these boots." Sven tied the laces together and hung them around his neck. "Thank you, Marcie. This could make all the difference."

He faced Lars and John. "Each of us should tie a clothes bundle to our backs, and then we need to head out. The storm isn't letting up."

After kissing Micah on his chubby, pink cheek, he held the baby toward Marcie.

Micah leaped into her arms. "Mama. Mama," he whimpered.

"Your daddy is going to go get her." She patted his little back. "Let's go play with Katie." She planted a quick kiss on her husband's lips and cast a worried glance at the darkening sky. "Be careful," she whispered before disappearing into the house with Micah in her arms.

Sven tied the rope around his waist and handed the rope to Lars who did the same. "Tie yourself to the rope, John. The three of us will stick together. We'll spool out one rope at a time, and tie the next one when we get to the end. Keep your gloves on even when tying the rope. Fingers freeze at this temperature. Don't remove them for any reason."

Lars slapped his brother on the back, "We'll get her. Caroline and the kids both."

Closing his eyes, Sven stood still. He needed to be calm. He needed the whirling of his head and the churning of his stomach to stop. He needed to get to Caroline. "I can't lose her again. I can't." He tucked the top of his gloves under the sleeves of his coat. "I pray you're right."

"I'm ready," John said. The men looped coils of rope around their arms and stepped from the porch.

"Loki," Sven called. The big husky sat at his feet, tail swishing, eyes focused on his master's face. Sven put his hand in his pocket and removed Caroline's winter scarf from his pocket. The scarf she'd worn every day save this one. Holding the item under Loki's nose, he gave the command. "Find Caroline, Loki. Find Caroline."

Loki sniffed at the scarf. He buried his face in the brightly colored yarn and rubbed his nose left and right. He turned toward the school, spun in a circle, and barked.

"Go, Loki. Go." The dog dashed forward, turned to wait for the slower men, and dashed again.

The ice fell faster, stinging, burning, lacerating their faces. Sven bent his head down to avoid the brutal onslaught of frozen knives of ice. They reached the end of the first rope, and John tied the second.

Sven lifted his head. The world was a single color—white. Tree branches coated with ice and icicles hung heavy toward the ground. A large branch snapped under the load and crashed to earth. He shook his head. He'd never seen the like. They would need to stay out in the open to avoid being hit by falling boughs. Looked like there was more than one way for a man to die on a day like today. He tipped his hat at the tree. Lars scowled at the fallen branch. He nodded his understanding.

Loki barked and twirled circles in the snow. He wanted them to hurry.

A piece of ice slithered past the collar of his coat, melted, and created a trail of ice water inching its way down his back. He shuddered. Lord have mercy. This hell of a storm made snow look like child's play. He risked a glance at the shuttered sun. Forty minutes. Maybe fifty since they left John's house. On a clear day, the school was an easy thirty-minute walk. They were slowed by the pelting ice, their heavy loads, and the necessity to stop to tie the ends together, but they should reach the destination soon. He hoped Caroline waited inside the building. If she took those children out on her own, he'd tan her hide. Sven swallowed a lump of despair. If she'd tried such a fool thing, he wouldn't have the chance.

Loki returned, grabbed Sven's sleeve in his teeth, and pulled. He lurched forward and struck his head on the side of a building. Loki tugged again, and Sven let himself be pulled until his foot bumped wood. Kneeling down, he patted the ground. A step, it was the first step into the school.

Sven shouted, "We're here," over the wicked whistle of the wind.

John fell as he hit the first stair, and they were all dragged to their knees. They rose and straggled to the door. Sven shoved the door open. The three men burst into the room bringing cold and ice and relief with them.

"Pa, Pa," two voices shouted, and two small bodies separated from the desperate little group huddled in front of the smoldering fire in the stove.

"Ava, Adam. Are you all right?" John pulled them tight to his body.

"Caroline?" Sven called. He pulled the scarf from his neck, whipped the hat from head, and wiggled his fingers from his gloves.

"I'm here, Sven," she replied. "Thank God you came for us. I planned to wait a few minutes more before trying it on my own."

"I'll always come for you, sweetheart. Always." Sven crossed to the chair where Caroline sat with a wide-eyed Lillian on her lap. The MacGregor boys huddled together at her feet. Their breaths made little puffy clouds in the frigid air. "I'm glad you didn't go out with these children on your own. It's far too dangerous out there. I always want you to stay put and wait for me." He didn't mean to scold, but his voice was harsh even to his own ears.

"I'd used all the wood. That's the last log finishing now. I couldn't just sit here and let the children freeze." Indignation saturated every word.

Sven knelt beside the chair and took one of her hands between his. "I know. I was frightened, is all." He leaned until his forehead rested against hers and the very air they breathed united. "We need to get all of you to safety."

"You boys all right?" The MacGregor boys shivered with the cold, and their teeth chattered. Sven laid a reassuring hand on their small shoulders.

"Yes, sir, but we're cold, and we sure would like to get on home." Eli MacGregor responded. His brother nodded so hard his hair flew.

Sven untied the clothes bundle from his back and motioned for the other men to do the same. "Mrs. Wayne sent warm clothes. Let's look through and get everyone bundled up."

Caroline sorted the garments and distributed them to the children. When she was done, they were covered head to foot.

"Marcie sent these for you." Sven handed her the long woolen underclothes and heavy boots.

"Lars, you take the lead on the way back. Adam and Ava will walk behind you. John will be next. The MacGregor boys follow with Caroline behind them. I'll carry Lillian and be last in line." He scanned the group with solemn eyes. "Now, do not take your hand off the rope. Under no circumstances are you to take your hand off the rope."

"Good plan, Sven. We can keep watch on the children this way," John moved his twins until they stood in front of him. "Line up and put your gloves on."

Lars moved to the front and prepared to open the door. "Ready?"

The line moved like a snake toward the door. "Caroline, where are your gloves?"

"There weren't enough. It's more important that the children wear them," she explained.

He pulled his gloves off and handed them to his wife. "Put these on."

"What about you?" she asked.

Sven gripped her upper arm and moved to her side. He delivered a firm spank to her bottom. "Do not argue. We need to get moving. Put on the gloves."

Caroline blushed deep pink, but her hands slid into Sven's large gloves without further protest.

"We're ready, Lars. Open the door." Sven called to his brother.

A rush of cold air and ice blew into their faces as they stepped from the safety of the school into the whirling storm.

Sven held Lillian with one arm and the rope with the other. His eyes scanned the group ahead, sweeping constantly, making sure no one dropped the rope and wandered onto the range.

At first his hand burned with the cold, but he had to hold the little girl. He had to hold the rope. He marched on.

It was a relief when the pain was replaced with numb absence. His hand was gone. Disappeared. But he held the rope, held the child, and walked on.

"We made it," Lars shouted.

The door to the Wayne house flew open and Marcie pulled them one at a time into the warmth, safety and comfort of the house.

She had pans of warm water ready, and she dipped hands into it and examined them one by one. Faces were bathed and ears checked.

Sven plunged his hands into the warm liquid.

"How does that feel?" Marcie asked.

"Warm," Sven replied.

Marcie cradled his hand. Her eyebrows lowered, and her lips

pressed into a short straight line. "Didn't you wear gloves?" she demanded.

"There weren't enough," Sven explained.

"What is it?" Caroline joined them. "What's the matter?"

"I don't like the looks of Sven's hands," she sighed. "Sven, keep your hands in the water. Move your fingers. Get the blood flowing. Restore circulation." She cocked her head and listened. "Micah and Katie are awake."

The two toddlers straggled into the room dragging their blankets behind them.

"Mama, mama." Micah held his arms up in the universal toddler signal for up.

Caroline hoisted him to her hip and rubbed her cheek over his white blond hair. "What did you say?"

Micah pressed his face into her bosom and burrowed. Micah raised his head and rewarded her with an impish grin. One she had witnessed on her husband's face more than once.

He patted her breast. "Mama," he announced.

"Da?" Micah pointed at Sven.

"I'm all right, son. Just washing my hands." Sven smiled at the boy. He'd rather be holding the two of them in his arms and not sitting here with his hands in a pan of water like an invalid.

"Everyone sleeps here tonight," Marcie declared. "It is too dangerous to go out, and I want to monitor everyone's health. Freezing temperatures are dangerous." She sent a worried glance at Sven's hands as they lay waxy and pale in the pan of warm water. "John, please find bedding for our guests."

"All right," John replied. He looked at each person in the room. "When Marcie's orders concern health or medicine, we always do as she says."

"I'll help." Sven began to rise from his chair.

"Keep your hands in the warm water," Marcie ordered.

Lars cleared his throat before speaking. "I'll help." He followed John from the room.

Sven listened as John brought order to the night. "We'll make a bed for the MacGregor boys on the floor of Adam's room. Lillian can sleep with Ava. We'll put together a pallet for Sven, Caroline and Micah. Lars, you can sleep on the couch if it's long enough."

"Thank you," Lars replied. "That will be fine."

"Caroline, come help me put a meal together." Marcie peered again at Sven's pale hands before turning her frown toward the door.

Just as he was about to abandon the warm water on his own, Caroline appeared in the door.

"Dinner's ready." She handed him a towel. "Thank God you came for us today, Sven. You saved us."

"I'll always come for you. Don't ever doubt it." Sven dried his hands before dragging his wife into a tight embrace. "I had help today. Lars and John came, too." He stepped back. "Do you think you can give Lars another chance? At the first sign of trouble, he was at my side. I know he's caused a lot of hurt over the years, but maybe he's changed. I believe in forgiveness, sweetheart. I can't give up on him, and we both know the blessing of a second chance."

"I don't know." Caroline stood on tiptoe to swish a soft, warm kiss over her husband's lips. "I'm afraid he'll disappoint you again or betray you." Her words were a soft hiss.

"Idiot that I am, I'll forgive him again," he whispered.

"You are too kind for you own good." Caroline leaned into his body.

He tucked her under his arm. "Let's go eat. It's been one hell of a day, and I'm hungry as a bear."

"It has definitely been one hell of a day," Caroline agreed.

Sven laid a warning swat on her sweet bottom.

"What's that for?" She wiggled away.

"You know better than to swear," he responded.

"You said it first."

"Well, I should watch my language, too, but ladies are not allowed to swear." Sven reminded his tiny wife.

"Hardly seems fair," she complained with a sassy toss of her head. She had let her hair down so it would dry. It lay against her back in a thick curtain of black silk. He longed to hold it in his hand and lift it to reveal the soft skin at the back of her neck. First, he had to set things straight.

"Maybe not, but it's the way of things. Try it again and see where it gets you." His eyes glittered a warning. "Perhaps I should close the door and make myself clear. I wouldn't mind a look at the bottom I saved today."

"You wouldn't spank me here." Her eyes snapped with her sharp retort. Her voice crackled with disobedience.

"If you need to be spanked, I will. Do you?" he asked. "Do you need to be spanked or will you watch your language and behave?"

"I'll behave." The belligerent tone disappeared.

"I'm glad, sweetheart. I'd rather have dinner." Sven took her hand into his.

He was mighty happy the argument had ended. He still couldn't feel his fingers, although the palm of his hand tingled with returning blood. Spanking might have proved difficult, but he would have found a way – a wooden spoon or a hairbrush would do the trick.

"Yes, sir," he mumbled. "Where there's a will; there's a way."

# CHAPTER 16

CAROLINE

*C*aroline slept sandwiched between her husband and her son on the floor of the Wayne home. A fine sheet of perspiration coated her forehead and a bead of sweat made a slow trail between her breasts. Mercy, it was hot.

She sat up slowly. Micah lay to her left. His little diaper covered bottom waved in the air, and his thumb was planted between rosy lips. Caroline sighed. He was a beautiful child, strong and healthy. He'd be eighteen months in a few days. Since she spent her days at school, she only nursed him at bedtime now, and he drank from a cup like a big boy with obvious pride. But the urge to hold him to her breast this morning caused her small mounds to become hard and full. If Sven and the other men hadn't come for them when they did, they would have died. Because of Sven, she was blessed with another day. Another opportunity to hold her son and love his father.

Caroline turned to her right and laid a hand on Sven's arm. She jerked back as if scalded before coming to her knees for a closer look at her husband. She laid her hand on his forehead. He didn't move. He didn't respond. That was why she had been so hot. Sven was a blazing furnace.

Marcie emerged from her bedroom. A robe tied loosely over her nightgown. Her curly hair surrounded her face in a fuzzy halo. She gave Caroline a little smile, "Time to start breakfast. We have a full house this morning." Marcie bent to rekindle the stove.

"Marcie," Caroline croaked.

Marcie turned at the sound of her distress. As midwife and physician to the town, she recognized the sound.

"Sven's burning up, Marcie." She turned a pale, pleading face toward her friend.

"Let me see." Marcie hurried to the pallet, and pulled the blankets down to reveal Sven's hands. "Oh Lord, I was afraid of this." She held Sven' hand and turned it over for closer inspection.

Several of his fingers were a waxy, lifeless color. Fluid filled blisters appeared on these fingers as well. His nails were a deep bluish black.

Caroline flinched. "Lord have mercy," she whispered.

Sven's eyes, still dazed with sleep, opened. The pair of women leaning over his body brought him further awake. "What's the matter?"

Bang. A fist hit the front door with vigorous intent. Bang. Bang.

"I'll get it," John said as he entered the room still buttoning his shirt. He opened the door before another knock woke the sleeping children.

"My boys here?" Jeb MacGregor whisked through the door shotgun gripped in his hand. Dark circles under his eyes spoke of a sleepless night, and his usual wild looks had turned murderous.

Before John could answer, the two boys burst into the room and ran into their father's embrace. He grabbed a boy in each arm as John pried the shotgun from his fingers.

"Mr. Nielson, Mr. Wayne and another Mr. Nielson came for us

yesterday. We were mighty scared, Pa, but we were brave," Eli assured his father.

"That they were," John agreed.

"I thank you, John," MacGregor released one son long enough to shake hands. "I knew I couldn't make it to town in that storm. In all my years, I'd never seen one that bad. I spent the night praying my boys had made it to safety."

He looked over at the two women and Sven huddled together on the floor. Sven's hands lay on top of the blanket like two injured birds fallen from the sky. MacGregor's face turned to gray.

"Preacher, you been frostbit. I seen that before, and I'm sorry for it." His mouth turned down in a mournful grimace. "I'll take my boys and head home. You let me know if I can help any, but that usually fixes itself or it don't." He patted each of his sons on the shoulder. "Gather your things," he ordered.

When the door shut behind them, Sven spoke. "I've seen this before, too. Minnesota winters bring blistering cold."

Marcie gave his hands a careful inspection. "You three stay here today, so I can keep a watch on your hands." She stood and smoothed her robe. "First, let's have breakfast."

While they cooked, Lillian's parents arrived and covered their daughter in kisses and warm clothes. After many, many thanks, handshakes and hugs, they took their leave.

John and Lars spent the morning doing chores and seeing to John's horses. Marcie declared it too cold for the children to play outside, and they settled into games in Adam's room. After dinner and amid protest, Micah and Katie lay down for their afternoon naps. John and Lars played chess while Caroline helped Marcie with her mending and preparations for the evening meal. Through all of this, Sven lay, fevered, eyes sunken in dark circles, on the pallet in front of the fire with Loki by his side. Caroline brought water time and time again, and Lars would lift his shoulders so he could drink. After each attempt to keep her husband hydrated, she and Lars exchanged desperate, unhappy looks.

With supper behind them, dishes done, and children in their beds for the night, Marcie cleared her throat. "We need to wake Sven. I'd like to explain our options."

Lars gave his brother a gentle shake followed by a not so gentle shove. "Sven, wake up. We need to talk." Sven nodded, and Lars helped him into a rocker next to the fire.

"Sven, you have third degree frostbite in three of your fingers," Marcie began. "Lars and Caroline, pay close attention. I'm not sure Sven will stay completely awake and understand the choices. You need to help him." They watched as Sven slumped sideways in the big chair.

"All right, Marcie, I'm listening," Caroline said. Lars nodded and crossed muscular arms across his chest.

Marcie continued. "That means that three of Sven's fingers are dead. In my opinion, the circulation will not return. You can see the black areas on the index finger of his right hand and the little and ring finger on his left."

Caroline surveyed these fingers, blackened and swollen, and moaned.

"There is a remote possibility blood flow will return, but it is a very small chance." Marcie looked first at Sven, then Caroline, and then Lars. "In my opinion," she concluded.

"Please, Marcie, yours is the only opinion we have. What can be done?" Caroline begged for an answer, a solution, a miracle.

"We can wait. It's possible his fingers will fall off on their own. It's called self -amputation. My worry, my fear, is infection. If we wait and infection sets in, it could poison his blood. Worse case is gangrene. Now, I don't know if that will happen, but it's a definite possibility." She waited a bit before plowing forward. "Here's the choice. I can amputate those three fingers. There is always a chance of infection, but I will do all in my power to avoid it. The other choice, as I said, is to wait. But if he develops an infection, if it turns into gangrene, he might lose his entire hand or both hands. At that point, I would have to remove all damaged tissue and gangrene spreads quickly.

"Oh no, no, no." Caroline's words mingled with sobs.

John stood in the shadow by the hearth. He stepped forward. "I just want to add that my wife is a skilled physician. She saved Amanda's life and my leg when I was shot some years back. Sven is in good hands."

Caroline leaned close to her husband. "Did you hear, Sven? What's your choice?"

He opened fever filled eyes. "I heard most. Need my hands," he mumbled before slipping into uneasy slumber.

"Lars, what should we do?" Caroline's frantic voice echoed in the still room. She turned her tear-stained face toward Marcie. "If it were John, what would you do?"

"Amputate. The risk of waiting is too great and too uncertain," Marcie replied.

"I say let's not risk infection. Let Marcie amputate those three fingers." Lars spoke with certainty. "Sven can make do without a few fingers, but his entire hand..." He shook his head in sad denial.

"All right. Do it, Marcie. Please." Caroline sank to her knees and laid her head on her husband's knee. "Amputate."

Marcie transformed before her eyes into a woman of purpose and authority. "John, you will administer the ether. Lars, we will need you to hold his hand still. Even under anesthetic, he may jerk."

"What can I do?" Caroline enquired.

"You, my dear, may start water to boil." Marcie swept from the room and was heard rummaging in her closet.

"Lars, help me move the table into our bedroom. Sven will lay on it during the surgery." The two men lifted the large wooden table and carted it from the room.

When Sven lay with his shirt off and a blanket tucked under his arms, Marcie dropped gleaming knives into the roiling water. "Come kiss your husband good-night, Caroline. He's going to be fine."

"I love you, Sven. Sleep well." Tears fell in a steady stream as she stumbled from the room.

Before the door closed, she heard Marcie's instructions. "Five drops, John. He's very large. Three more if he begins to wake."

Loki whined at the closed door, then growled, before dropping to his belly. He lay his head between giant paws and stared at the barrier of wood.

Caroline bent to stroke his thick fur. "He'll be all right, Loki. We have to wait out here." The big dog heaved a tremendous sigh, but his shoulders relaxed a bit.

When Micah woke and stumbled, sleep-addled, from his bed, Caroline unbuttoned her blouse and let the child suckle. Taking comfort, each from the other, they slept before the smoldering fire.

"Water." Sven's voice was a dry croak. He lay with his arms crossed on his chest. Both hands swaddled in large, bulky bandages.

Loki lay on her husband's other side. He rose to his feet and stared down into Sven's face, tongue hanging, tail wagging, ears up and alert.

"Good boy, Loki." Sven managed to rub his back with his forearm. Loki returned to his favorite spot – glued to his master's side.

Caroline rose from the pallet, stepped over her sleeping son, and pumped water into a glass. Returning to her husband, she helped him lift his head and held the cold liquid to his lips. When he'd had enough, he nodded and laid his head on the sweat dampened pillow.

"Thank you, sweetheart. I'm still groggy from the ether," he mumbled, "but I'd like to sit in the rocker." He rose with trembling limbs and sank onto the wooden seat. Loki followed and lay on his feet.

Opening his arms, Caroline crawled onto his lap and curled into his chest. Her husband enfolded her in his arms, careful not to bump his injured hands, and cradled her against him.

"I'll be all right," he reassured her.

"Thank God," Caroline replied. "I couldn't live without you

again. I had resigned myself to life alone, but now I've found you." Her voice dissolved in an onslaught of tears.

Marcie emerged from her room and rushed to Sven's side. "How do you feel?"

"My hands are a mite sore." He lifted the bandaged appendages.

"If you rest your elbows on the arms of the chair and hold your hands in the air as much as possible, it will help reduce the swelling," she instructed.

Sven reluctantly released his wife and did as Marcie said.

"I'd like you to stay here today. If you don't have a fever and the pain is bearable, you can return home this evening. That is, if Caroline thinks she can take care of Micah, the house, and you until your wounds heal," Marcie said.

Sven interrupted, "How long before I can work?"

Marcie's lips were a stern line. "I can reduce the bandaging in a few days. At that point, I want you to exercise your fingers. You don't want to lose range of motion, even in the stumps of the missing ones. I'd say about three weeks before the wounds are healed or close to it. You can begin to use your hands then, but carefully at first."

Caroline closed her eyes and fought the rising nausea burning the back of her throat. Stumps, now there was an ugly word. Jagged, ragged wood stabbing accusing fingers at the sky rose in her mind. She forced herself to look at Sven's bandaged hands. Marcie would have been neat and precise. She knew her well enough to know that. Maybe the stumps would not be ugly. Caroline turned her imagination to fresh cut trees. The ones that left behind the tree's history in concentric circles and blessed the air with the smell of fresh pine. Her husband's frustrated voice broke through her reverie.

"But I have furniture orders, and Caroline can't chop wood," Sven began.

"I can," Lars broke in.

Caroline's head snapped in her brother-in-law's direction. "What?"

"I can work on the furniture if Sven tells me what to do. I can chop wood, carry water, and help Caroline. Please, let me help," Lars' eyes glittered with a silent plea.

"Thank you, brother. That would be mighty good of you." Sven and Lars turned their identical ice blue eyes to her. They looked so hopeful her heart gave a painful squeeze.

Could she do it? She had a lifetime of resentment built up and aimed at Lars. Time after time, he'd caused trouble, interfered, dragged Sven into one mess after the next. But in all that time, Sven never lapsed, never stopped loving his brother, never quit seeing the best in him when all others abandoned hope.

Well, it was one of the things she loved most about her husband after all. He hadn't given up on her either, and she knew with certainty he never would. His love was a rock. His faith a mountain. His loyalty a harbor where he sheltered, nourished and sustained those he held dear.

She would not deny that depth of faith and goodness. To do so would be like denying the renewal of spring. Spring. A person couldn't help but love that rebirth when little green shoots poked their heads through warm earth and baby animals cavorted with awkward, long-legged clumsiness. Sven's belief in his brother was that deep, that fresh, that hopeful, that long-legged.

She didn't have much faith in Lars. Caroline had given that up long ago. She would keep a close watch on that brother-in-law of hers. At the first sign of trouble, she would send him on his way. She would honor Sven's bottomless well of forgiveness, as long as Lars deserved it.

"Thank you, Lars, we would appreciate your help," Caroline said with as much enthusiasm as she could garner.

Sven was off and away. "We can put a cot in Micah's room for you. I'm going to need help dressing, and, well, with more private matters," he blushed bright red. "I'd rather not have my wife…"

147

Lars saved his brother from his tongue-tied embarrassment. "I'll set up a cot this afternoon and start the fire. No sense going home to a stone-cold house."

When Marcie declared Sven fit to return home later that day, they entered an enticing room of crackling warmth filled with the aroma of fresh coffee.

"I was just going to fill the wood box," Lars headed toward the door with the eagerness of an overgrown puppy. "Then you let me know what else needs doing." He stopped at the door and turned serious eyes on Caroline. "Anything. Just ask."

"Thank you, Lars," Caroline replied. A hard lump in her chest melted a tiny bit. There was a minute lessening and a single bead of moisture slid down the windowpane of her resentment. "I will."

Caroline set Micah on the floor, and he toddled off. The boy's steps were still a little unsure, but every day, no, every hour, he became steadier, faster, more confident. He set a brisk clip across the room and settled on his bottom in front of the box filled with blocks his father had sanded to silky smoothness. Loki followed in his wake dropping to his belly next to the child.

Sven turned glowing, suspiciously bright eyes to his wife. "Caroline, I do believe he's a changed man. I think my brother…"

"Let's not get ahead of ourselves. I agree he seems sincere, but the emphasis is on seems. Let's wait and see if the change is from his heart." Caroline paused as a flash of pain crossed his handsome face. She put her arms around him. "I just don't want him to hurt you again. That's all. I'm willing to give him a chance, but…"

"I know, sweetheart. His history is long and painful. Thank you for giving him, us, this chance." He patted her back with an awkward thump.

Caroline pointed at the big rocker. "Sit down, Sven, and keep your hands elevated like Marcie said."

"All right," he grumbled, "but don't get used to ordering me around, wife. I won't have it."

She waited, hands on hips, until her husband sank into the big chair before moving into the kitchen. She had supper to tend to.

"Do you hear me, Caroline?" Sven called. "I won't have it."

"I hear you," she called over her shoulder. Turning back, she saw Sven rest his head on the back of the rocker and close his eyes.

She'd tread lightly, but Sven needed to recuperate, and he wouldn't take to it. He'd pull at the bit every step of the way.

Well, she'd driven headstrong horses. She'd corralled recalcitrant children. She could keep one husband in line.

Or die trying. She rolled her eyes in a manner sure to earn her a swift spank if her husband was not snoring in the large rocker. This was one tussle she aimed to win.

# CHAPTER 17

SVEN

*C*aroline swept into the room on a cloud of cool air. "I saw Marcie walking up the street when I left the Mercantile. Has she been here? Did she look at your hands?" The words emerged in a rushing torrent.

Sven laughed. "She was, and she did." He held up his unbandaged hands and wiggled his seven fingers.

His wife hurried to his side and took his hands in both of hers, turning them this way and that. "They look wonderful," she pronounced.

He knit his brow and studied his transformed appendages. "Well, that might be going a bit too far, but they'll do." Sven pulled her onto his lap. "I can hold my child, cut my own meat, build furniture and spank a little bottom if I need to." He waggled his eyebrows. "One little lady I know has been mighty bossy of late. I'd warn her to change her tune before I have to put that particular talent to the test." He nuzzled her neck to take the sting from his words.

Lars cleared his throat. "I can go for a walk," he offered.

"No need, brother," Sven replied.

He surveyed his wife from head to toe, raised an eyebrow in his brother's direction, and shifted in his chair. The air crackled with sudden unease. Both men studied the contents of their coffee cups as if the answer to the meaning of life lay buried in the dark depths of steaming liquid.

Caroline's head swiveled from one Nordic face to the other. "What have you two been up to?" she asked. "You look like you've been caught with your hand in the cookie jar."

Sven considered his raven-haired wife. "We've been talking."

"About?" she prompted.

"About the past. About the future," Sven said.

Lars lifted his hands and let them drop to the table before speaking. "Caroline, I know you have no reason to trust me, but I'd appreciate it if you'd hear me out."

"All right." Reluctance tinged with distrust swirled like dust devils around those two words.

Sven flinched but gave his brother an encouraging nod.

"Well," Lars lifted his eyes from his coffee cup. "Well, you've probably been wondering why I've been standing across the street all this time."

"Yes," Caroline replied, "it did seem odd."

"Well," he began again, "I was thinking. Thinking about Ma, and Sven, and Cold Spring, and why I've been so much trouble." Lars brought the cup to his lips and sipped. "I think I found some answers. I never stopped before to think. I was always moving, drinking, running. Standing across the street, watching you and Sven and Micah, gave me time to think."

Sven pulled out a chair and motioned to his wife. "Sit down, sweetheart. Come sit by me."

Caroline's face was rigid. Her mouth a tight little line, but she lowered her bottom onto the chair and waited.

"Now I know this doesn't excuse my behavior, but I remember

before Pa died. Sven and me, well, we were just two boys. He'll always be five years older, of course, but we were kids. Sharing a room, doing chores, catching hell sometimes. Ma would take a wooden spoon to our backsides or Pa would take us to the woodshed. Now, that was a place you didn't want to go. I can tell you that for a fact." He winced at the memory of those long ago encounters.

"Those visits were memorable," Sven agreed.

"Then Pa died," Lars continued. "Things changed. Of course, they changed. How could they not? But the thing was Ma made Sven the man of the house. Those were her exact words. *Sven, you are now the man of the house.* Sven, being Sven, took that duty to heart."

Sven dragged Caroline's chair closer and draped an arm around her small shoulders. She didn't trust Lars, and she had good reason, but he hoped she heard his story with an open heart and mind. Heaven only knew why, but even after all the trouble his brother had caused, he couldn't stop caring for him and wanting him in his life. He lifted his wife from her chair and set her in his lap, enfolded her in his arms and placed a kiss on the top of her silky, black hair. He nodded at Lars to continue.

"This next part is pure selfish, and the only excuse I have is that I was a kid. But, where did that leave me? If Sven was man of the house, what was I? Not only had I lost my pa; I lost my brother. Ma let him stay up late and sit with her by the fire discussing the farm, the harvest, the need to hire extra help. They talked about me. I'd lay in the dark and listen and resentment festered. Now I understand Ma's loneliness, her need for someone to talk to, but her promotion of Sven to my sort of pa left me alone, resentful, angry." He raised his shoulders and let them fall. "That was when I started raising hell – at home, at church, at school – anywhere I could misbehave, I did. It went from disobedience to defiance. By the time I was sixteen, I was breaking the law. I guess I wanted attention, especially from my brother, and I got it. He would come to my rescue. Promise the teacher or sheriff he would keep me out of trouble. I only got angrier. I wanted my brother to be my brother not my guardian."

"I can understand that, Lars. But letting Sven go to jail?" She shook her head. "How could you? After all he'd done for you?"

"I don't rightly know, Caroline, and I'm ashamed. I was just so damned angry all the time. When we were arrested, I thought, now Sven would get what he deserved for chasing after me all those years. I thought he would finally leave me alone and go back to being Ma's man of the house." Tears hovered unshed in Lars' pale eyes. "The worst was when I broke up your wedding. Pure meanness, Caroline, pure meanness. All I can do is beg your forgiveness. Rage at the world, at Sven, boiled over. Even after jail, he walked away the good brother, the golden boy. He was preaching; he had a son; he had you. And I was still the no-account troublemaker." A single tear slid down his cheek. Lars swiped at it with the cuff of his shirt.

Putting a finger under his wife's chin, Sven turned her head until he could look into her eyes. "Lars and I have been talking," he began. "You and I already decided to leave San Miguel."

"I know," Caroline whimpered, "but I hate to go."

Sven rubbed circles on her back. "I know, sweetheart, so do I, but it's for the best."

"I'm sorry," Lars croaked. "It's my fault."

"Yes, it is." Caroline flung the anger-soaked words. "We had a new start."

"Water under the bridge," Sven interrupted. He was aiming for reconciliation not recrimination. He took a deep breath. "I want Lars to come with us."

"What?" His wife's screech was painful and loud.

"Hush, you'll wake Micah," he cautioned.

"Go with us where? Have the two of you been plotting behind my back?" Her voice lowered, but he still didn't like her strident tone. It grated.

"You know I wouldn't do that. We've just been tossing some ideas around is all, but I'd appreciate it if you didn't hurl accusations," Sven cautioned. "I'd like you to listen with an open mind." He lifted one eyebrow until it disappeared under his hair. This particular look was often the harbinger of a spanking. He hoped it would gain her attention.

"All right. Tell me." A small sigh escaped her lips as his eyebrow resumed its normal height.

"Good girl." He patted her bottom. "You know I sold Ma's farm."

"Yes, I know," Caroline affirmed.

"The money is in the bank. Half of it belongs to Lars. Well, we were thinking that if we pooled our funds, we could all get a new start." Sven hurried on before his wife could lodge a protest. "First, we pack up my tools and travel to Abilene. We'll take the train to San Francisco. Lars and I," he motioned at his brother, "can buy a wagon, and we'll head north. Now, we studied the map, and we believe we are aiming for a place in Oregon called the Willamette Valley. But if we see something better on the way, we'll stop, but there's good farmland in that valley, sweetheart, rain but no big snow or ice storms." He shivered and gave his missing fingers a rueful consideration. "We'll build one house first and share it. When Lars finds himself a wife, we'll build another house." He laughed. "Everyone knows two women in one house is trouble." Sven's eyes sparkled and his voice rose with every revelation. "I can make furniture. We can raise crops and children." He stammered to a stop. "What do you think?"

"What do I think?" She repeated his question. "It sounds like you've already worked it out. Why ask me?" She turned her back to him.

"You know what happens when you shut me out, Caroline." Sven used one long finger to turn her face in his direction a second time. "Tell me, us, what you think. I don't want a resentful, angry wife. Either we all agree to the plan, or Lars takes his share of the money and goes his own way."

"How do you know he won't cause trouble again? Share our past with the new town? I don't want to spend my life looking for another new start." Caroline slipped Lars a heated glare.

"I won't. I swear. I won't," Lars said. "You don't have much reason to trust me, but I won't."

"Well, you're right about that. I don't have much reason to trust you," she said through gritted teeth.

"Forgive, sweetheart. Forgive. Please, don't make me choose between my brother and my wife. Selfish as I am, I want both," Sven pled. He knew, even as he said it, that it was a lot to ask. Caroline wanted, deserved, peace in her life and in her home.

"For you, Sven, I'll try." She wagged her index finger one, twice, three times at her brother-in-law. "Don't make me regret it, Lars, or I swear…"

"You won't." Lars rushed in with reassurance.

Caroline gave a nod. "About those children we plan to raise in Oregon. The first one is due in September, and I don't want to give birth in a wagon. When did you two fix on leaving?"

Sven stood and took his wife with him. "Micah's going to have a brother?" he stammered.

"Or a sister," she confirmed.

He kissed her with all the love and care and promise a man can put in a kiss. Setting her on her feet, he splayed his hand over her flat abdomen. "I won't miss a single minute this time."

Lars bounded around the table. "Congratulations, Sven." He pounded his brother's back in masculine pride at his accomplishment before placing a tender kiss on Caroline's cheek.

Sven pulled them both into a bear hug and squeezed. He was going to have it all – his brother, his wife, Micah, a baby. His heart was full to bursting, and he knew he owed thanks for this glorious bounty.

"Dear Lord," he began. Caroline and Lars stilled, waiting. "Thank you for the blessings you have bestowed upon us. Thank you for returning my brother. Thank you for giving me another chance to be Caroline's husband. Thank you for Micah and the child as yet unborn. Help us walk our path together, as a family." He paused and squeezed them a second time until Caroline groaned. "Sorry, sweetheart," he apologized. "Amen and Oregon or bust!"

Lars hooted before shouting the refrain. "Oregon or bust!"

A pause, brief but painful, ensued. Sven looked into his wife's uncertain eyes.

She shrugged before she echoed, "Oregon or bust!"

A little voice called from the other room, "Ogon bus."

Loki barked.

Caroline, Lars, and Sven laughed until tears ran down their cheeks, and they held their sides in breathless glee. It seemed they had reached agreement.

Oregon or bust!

# EPILOGUE

*Caroline* sat in the open window of the San Francisco hotel. Cool ocean breezes swept into the room bathing her in light mist. She closed her eyes and inhaled the salty air. After days on a hot train, the relief was welcomed and sweet.

Standing, she crept to the bed and pulled a light blanket over a sleeping Micah. She threw a shawl around her own shoulders and returned to her vigil. Cool was turning to cold as the afternoon wore on.

Lars and Sven left early that morning to purchase a wagon, horses and supplies for the journey north. She'd expected them back long ago. Sven had ordered her to stay in the room. A town full of sailors many months at sea was not safe.

Caroline patted her pregnant belly. She didn't think any man, no matter how many months at sea, would bother with a woman nearly eight months gone. The baby gave her a good kick. She leaned back, stretching as tall as she could to give the internal traveler more room.

Her back ached; her head hurt, and she was worried. Caroline closed her eyes. They'd intended to leave San Miguel in March, April at the latest. Then Granny Wilkins fell ill again, and she begged Sven to see her through her final days to her glory. In her heart, she knew Sven made the right choice. But Granny Wilkins and her feisty spirit fought death to the end. Just when the doctor thought she'd breathed her last, she'd sputter and gasp and that skinny chest would rise and fall, rise and fall. Sven had prayed at her grave the second week in July, and then they'd left both friend and foe behind in San Miguel.

It was the first week of August. The baby was due mid-September, and she didn't want to give birth in a wagon. She clenched her teeth until her jaw ached.

An indignant yell brought Caroline to the window. She leaned over the casement and craned her head right and left.

What in the world? Lars held a tight grip on a young boy's arm and every few steps he'd land a spank hard enough to lift the lad off his feet. Their voices drifted through the window.

"Stop your caterwauling," Lars growled.

"Let go of me, mister. You got no right!" The boy twisted and writhed, but Lars held firm.

"No right, huh? Like you had no right to my money?" he demanded.

Boots pounded up the stairs, and a key turned in the lock. Her husband entered with Loki at his heels. Lars followed with the scamp in tow.

"What do you think the sheriff would do if we turned you in? You ought to be thanking us instead of shrieking up a goddamned storm like a little girl. We could still do it. We could still let the law take care of a robber like you." Lars motioned at Sven. "You're lucky my brother is too kind-hearted for his own good. If it were up to me, you'd be cooling your heels in a cell."

That settled the kid some. He looked down at his feet and then peered up at the two large men. "Well, I guess you got the right of it. I don't want to go to jail, but that's because the Prescott's own that old marshal. He ain't worth a plug nickel, and he'd give me to Simon Prescott before the sun went down." He struggled for his freedom once more. "Turn me loose. I'll be on my way."

"Who are the Prescotts, and why would he turn you over to them?" Lars asked.

"Ain't none of your business." The rascal pulled his foot back and kicked Lars, hard, on his right shin. When Lars loosened his grip the kid squared up and kicked again. This blow was aimed between Lars' legs, and it would have met with success if Lars hadn't seen it coming and knocked the thief away.

"Why you little brat," Lars dragged the kid to the chair by the window where Caroline had rested. He pulled the boy over his lap and lit into his backside. "I'll teach you to fight dirty." He rained punishment onto that rascal's bottom until the kid quit his yelling and slumped over Lars' knee in defeat.

Caroline, Sven and Micah retreated across the room and watched in uncomfortable silence.

"Uncie Lar spank," Micah spluttered around his damp thumb.

"He did," Caroline agreed.

Lars stood the kid on his feet. "What's your plan? If we turn you loose, are you going to steal again?"

"You bastard," the boy said through gritted teeth, "you don't know nothing about who I am or what I got to do."

"Don't swear in front of my wife and son," Sven growled.

"You want another spanking?" Lars asked. "I got plenty more where that came from." He put large hands on the youngster's shoulders and shook.

"Lars, stop," Caroline shouted. "Look."

The kid's hat had been pulled down tight to his ears, but between the spanking and the shaking, it had fallen off. A long braid the color of flame swung free to the kid's waist. Escaped curls framed a pixie's face with bright green eyes and a generous sprinkling of freckles.

Lars stared.

Sven choked.

Caroline said, "He's a girl."

"Why are you dressed like a boy?" Lars asked.

"It was my disguise, and it was working. I need to get out of town before Simon Prescott finds me. Please. Let me go," she whimpered.

Lars looked at Sven and some agreement came to be in that glance.

"We can't let a woman loose on her own. It's not safe. We leave San Francisco in the morning. You can hide in our wagon until we're clear of the city. But," he stabbed a finger in her direction, "you are going to explain what this is about in the morning. When it's safe, you can be on your way. Is that understood?"

She gave a surly nod.

"Sorry, Sven, but I think the little gal will have to sleep with Caroline and Micah. We'll bunk in the other room. We'll leave Loki with the women. He'll guard them," Lars said. "If that's agreeable with Caroline," he added.

"It is," Caroline said.

"If you run away in the night, I'll find you," Lars warned. "That little spanking you just had will seem like a Sunday picnic, so don't try it."

"Well, now that's settled," Caroline said before smiling at the young woman. "We haven't been introduced. I'm Caroline Nielson. This is my husband, Sven. You've met his brother, Lars." She rolled her eyes in the big man's direction. "This young man," she patted her son's back, "is Micah and sitting by him is our dog, Loki. We're traveling to Oregon. What's your name?"

"Eleanor Montgomery but I go by Ellie," she said. She cast a plaintive look at Caroline. "I know you're trying to help me, but you'll be sorry. The deck's stacked for the Prescotts, and they don't never lose. You need to do yourself a favor and let me go." She scowled. "You seem like nice people, and I don't want to see you get hurt."

"You didn't think stealing our money would hurt? We need that cash to get us up north and settled." Lars turned at the door. His eyes glowed like they were lit from the inside. "Stay put, Ellie. We can't turn our backs on a woman in trouble. We'll talk tomorrow. You women lock this door."

The door closed with a decisive click.

"Stay put, Ellie Montgomery," Lars warned through the weathered wood. "Stay put, or else."

The women listened to his boots stamp down the hall.

"Lars and Sven are a mite protective," Caroline explained with a shrug of her shoulders, "but they are good men and mean well."

Ellie rubbed at her bottom. "He better not try that again if he knows what's good for him," she growled. "I ain't no little kid."

Caroline opened her chest and withdrew a nightgown. "Here," she extended the garment to her guest, "you can sleep in this. It doesn't fit me right now, anyway."

Ellie pulled the boy's shirt over her head and unwound the strip of material restraining her breasts. Undressed and unbound, with her hair brushed into a river of red flowing to her waist, she'd gone from a scrubby boy to a breathtaking beauty.

Caroline smiled.

Lars would not want to let loose of this fetching troublemaker. Ellie would call to every masculine need to protect, defend and claim in the man's body. After all the worry he'd caused, it would serve him right to tangle with this misbehaving miss. She rested her hand on the swell of her belly and laughed out loud.

The Lord had a way of delivering justice.

He surely did.

The End

# VICTORIA PHELPS

Victoria Phelps lives in northern California with her two best friends: her handsome husband and her Goldendoodle, Max. She has two daughters, two sons-in-law, four granddogs and one grandcat. That's a lot of fur!

Victoria, who has always loved the written word, taught literature and writing. Now that she has the opportunity to write full time, she is in wordsmith heaven. She enjoys playing tennis, quilting, and reading, reading, reading.

Don't miss these exciting titles by Victoria Phelps and Blushing Books!

*Texas Time Travel Series*
Home on the Range - Book One
Meeting John Wayne - Book Two
Wyld Woman - Book Three

*Lone star Love Series*
Troubled Water - Book One
Treasured - Book Two
The Teacher and the Preacher - Book Three

*Connect with Victoria Phelps:*
www.victoriaphelpsromance.com

CPSIA information can be obtained
at www.ICGtesting.com
Printed in the USA
LVHW092329160520
655731LV00001B/37